Rescued by the Space Marine

I0562269

Taylor Neptune

ISBN: 978-1634810524

Foreword

Alhmanics - malevolent dictators of Kador. They heavily polluted the planet and now extort the native Kadorians for their healing services to heal the damage caused by the pollution.

Father Aghi - a priest of middle rank.

Father Alois - head of the temple where Illary and Suyana are kept.

Illary - Kaley's middle sister, an imprisoned healer inside of an

Alhmanic temple. Her name means rainbow.

Kaley - the protagonist of Claim of the Alien God, married to God-King Jesaja.

kho bo cay - spicy beef jerky.

mi ga - egg noodle soup with chicken.

Pachakutek - the head of a growing rebel force intent on taking down the Alhmanics and restoring control of Kador to the Kadorians.

Phuoc - the space marine who saves Suyana. He's one of the

Yuenanren.

Qullqi - temple gossip and voluntary acolyte of the Alhmanics.

ruou - concentrated alcohol, somewhat like vodka, but made from rice.

spätburgunder - Intaran red wine which has some aphrodisiac properties.

Suyana - Kaley's youngest sister, another imprisoned healer. Her name means hope.

Waqar - a voluntary acolyte of the Alhmanics.

xocolatl - hot chocolate with peppermint and some other aromatic herbs in it.

Xun - pronounced "soon." A space marine for Kandalph Space Marines, Inc. He came from a troubled past and has some reservations about his job.

Zhongguo - Xun's home planet.

Zhongguoren - Xun's race.

Zhongwen - Xun's language, though most Zhongguoren use Standard.

Naked Rituals

Illary

"You wanted to see me, Father?"

"Come in, child." Father Alois motioned for her to approach his desk.

"Am I in trouble, sir?"

He arched a brow. "Is there something that you've done that merits punishment?"

Illary quickly shook her head.

"No, sir." She suppressed a

shiver. Father Alois was always very severe with his punishments; the Alhmanics were not merciful people, and the last time that she'd transgressed in their eyes, they'd kept her on half rations for a week.

For a normal person, it would've caused mild hunger and fatigue. For a healer that used a ton of energy, it had pushed her to the brink of collapse. They hadn't reduced her duties when she was given half rations. When they weren't looking, her little sister Suyana had healed her, keeping her alive. Illary didn't want to think about what would happen to Suyana if she was left alone in the temple with the Alhmanics.

"Are you happy here, Illary?"

Illary knew what the answer was. She also knew that she would be punished if she told the truth, so she told the right lie.

"Of course, Father Alois."

"Good, child." He cleared his throat. "I believe that your nineteenth birthday was yesterday?"

"Yes, sir." Suyana had sneaked a little bit of extra food from a sympathetic kitchen worker in honor of her birthday, something that could earn all three of them "purification," also known as corporal punishment. Illary knew that Suyana shouldn't have done it, but she'd been grateful for the gesture anyway. It was a far cry from their childhood birthdays. They may not have had tremendous wealth, but their mother had always ensured that the day was special.

He looked at her breasts,

concealed by the shapeless burlap sacks that abraded their skin and itched like crazy. Illary shifted in her seat a little bit and crossed her arms.

"I believe that it's time for you to move to the next step of your training," Father Alois told her.

"Training?" She hadn't had any training for a long time. The basic tenets of the Alhmanic religion were easy to grasp; she'd learned healing at her mother's knee, though Kaley had always been the best at it.

"Yes. Now that you're old enough,

you can learn the naked rituals that will increase your healing powers tenfold."

She did not like the grin on his face one bit. She wasn't an idiot; she knew that there weren't any naked rituals in the Alhmanic tradition.

Staring at one of the heavy books behind his desk, she pulled it off of the shelf with her telekinesis. It wasn't all that reliable, but today it was working. The book made a loud thump when it fell, causing Father Alois to turn around for a split second.

Illary took the opportunity to reach around the desk and flick the switch that was kept under it. Alarms blared all across the temple, so Illary fled from his office as if pursued by a tiger, her heart pounding from her narrow escape.

Running

Illary

Illary ran through the hallways, ignoring how much the sound was making her ears hurt. The alarm bell echoed throughout the hallway, the sound bouncing off of the walls and becoming even louder. She was running in the opposite direction of the Mothers, the ones who shepherded the faithful. They gave her the evil eye, but she moved steadily towards the standard rendezvous point that was a safe distance away from the temple, in a small garden off to the side.

It was really meant for kitchen staff, since the kitchen was at the back and it was impractical for people to go through the whole temple if it was burning down. She would be safe there, and she could pretend that she, like the rest of the people, had no idea what was going on. If she looked for the best case scenario, she might be able to swipe some food while she was running through.

She was lucky. There was a big tray of bread rolls that were cooling on a rack. She grabbed one and began eating it quickly. The kitchen staff wouldn't begrudge her, but if one of the Fathers saw her, there'd be hell to pay. She ate it before anybody could take it away from her. The Fathers had learned early on that starving Illary and Suyana was the fastest way to make them comply with orders, no matter how distasteful.

Illary was finally in the side garden with everyone else. They could see that she was eating bread, but none of them said a word. Most of them were sympathetic Kadorians, but they infrequently stuck out their necks to smuggle food to Illary and Suyana. The sisters were kept under constant guard, which was why today was a rare opportunity.

Illary headed towards the back of the garden. She wasn't tall, which meant that she could blend in with the other Kadorians. She would have a few blessed moments of peace.

She nearly groaned when she got to the back and saw another temple acolyte there.

"Hi, Illary!" Qullqi chirped. "What are you doing back here?"

"Uh, I was in the back of the temple when the alarm bells sounded." The excuse sounded completely lame to Illary's ears, but Qullqi accepted the explanation without a question.

"Did you hear about what

happened with Waqar? She was found in the incense storage room with Father Aghi! Can you believe that they were totally horizontal when it happened?"

Qullqi kept chattering on, but Illary blocked her out. She didn't care about temple gossip. Unlike Illary, Qullqi was here by choice. She'd chosen to ally herself with the most powerful force on Kador, the Alhmanics. They ruled everything now, so the surest way to ensure that you had a place to sleep and food to eat was to work for them. Qullqi could leave whenever she wanted; Illary envied her freedom, but Qullqi squandered her time away by constantly keeping tabs on everyone else.

Illary realized that she was also probably fodder for Qullqi's rumor mill. She shivered when she thought of Qullqi broadcasting that she was found horizontal with Father Alois, the head priest. She didn't want to learn any naked rituals, thank you very much. She didn't know what kind of repercussions there might be, but she hoped that Father Alois would let it drop.

The alarm bells finally stopped blaring, and the kitchen staff went inside to resume their duties. Illary headed straight for her room, hoping to find Suyana there.

Peril

Illary

Illary walked quickly through the hallways, but she couldn't run without attracting attention. She opened the curtain leading to her room and, to her immense relief, found her little sister sitting on their shared bed.

"Where were you?" Suyana asked, her lower lip quivering. "I didn't see you at the rendezvous point. I looked and looked. Father Alois kept looking for you, too, and neither of us could find you."

"I wasn't there," Illary said. "I went to the alternate one."

"Oh."

Illary swallowed hard. She didn't want to do this, but she had no choice. "Suyana," Illary whispered, "we've got to run away. Kaley had the right idea when she left, and we've got to go."

"What's wrong?" Suyana asked, trembling. She hadn't had the luxury of the worry-free childhood that Kaley had enjoyed; Suyana, though not too much younger, had been very young when their father had died in an Alhmanic mine and their mother had been left to raise them alone.

Illary hated saying it, but Suyana was 18 now, and she had a right to know. "I think that Father Alois wants my body." That was the lowest-key way of saying it that she could think of. And Suyana's eyes were wide. She knew what Illary meant.

"What can we do?"

"I've been trying to figure a way out for years. I have a plan. Will you help me?"

Suyana nodded quickly.

"Let's try something. Give me your hands." Suyana reached out to take Illary's hands. Kaley was the strongest of all of them, which was probably why she'd been able to get out, but Suyana and Illary's combined efforts should be enough to get them out.

"We've got to try to raise an obscuring and protective veil."

Closing their eyes, they both visualized a veil to cover and protect them. They wouldn't have enough energy to keep it up for long, but they just might be able to find a way to link together. Today was a practice run for their escape.

Illary tried to concentrate on the veil, but she was interrupted by her thoughts of her older sister. Kaley had been named by their father. Their mother had been absolutely wiped out by the birth, and they hadn't known the gender beforehand.

Their father had chosen Caollaidhe, an echo of his distant Releon heritage, and their mother had been irate when she'd woken up. She'd made them to change it to Kaley, at least, saying that their child would be a laughingstock if she couldn't even spell her own name.

And she'd also insisted on naming the subsequent children. Neither birth had been as strenuous as the first one, so she'd been fine and conscious when the babies were named. Illary was named for the rainbow, while Suyana was named for the hope that she inspired, even as the Alhmanics took over Kador.

Suyana was Illary's only hope now that the two of them were left on Kador. They didn't begrudge Kaley for getting out; the amount of healing they were forced to do was slowly draining them. One day soon, they'd be drained to the last drop.

Her concentration broke, which made the veil fall.

"Just be ready, Suyana." Her little sister's eyes were watery, but she nodded. Illary hugged her close, wishing that their circumstances were different. Suyana was 18, less than a year younger than Illary, but she was the baby of the family. They'd taken care of her as best they could, but she was rapidly approaching a point where Illary couldn't protect her anymore.

Suyana yawned a huge yawn.

"Go to sleep, Suyana."

"Okay." Suyana didn't need to be convinced. She turned over in their shared bed and closed her eyes.

Neither of them could sleep. Both of them tossed and turned all night, frightened by what their future might hold.

Early Morning Healing

Illary

The next morning, Illary felt a ball of dread in her stomach as she thought about running into Father Alois again. Would he let the matter drop? She hoped so, but she thought that it was unlikely.

She rolled over to shake Suyana's shoulder.

"Wake up, Suyana. We've got to go to the early morning healing ritual."

Suyana's eyes were half-closed as she fumbled around for her burlap dress. They had simple cotton dresses for nighttime, blessedly comfortable, but the Alhmanics believed in a constant battle for repentance and purification, a distance from earthly functions, so each day was spent in total discomfort. The Mothers and the acolytes wore burlap, though Illary had noticed that none of the Fathers did. Maybe they were already pure enough.

They went out the door and into the main area of the temple, following the crowd. Everybody was expected to attend the early morning ritual. If they didn't show up on time, they'd spend the rest of the day being purified.

The sickest Kadorians always came to the early morning ritual. Illary wished that she could tell them not to bother; the ritual was mostly for show. The amount of healing energy generated during the ritual was negligible. It couldn't actually help them heal at all.

But Illary didn't dare to speak up. She'd spent many years of her life in the temple under the thumb of the Alhmanic Fathers, and she knew better than to contradict them and the stories that they fed the Kadorian population. They'd drained as much money as they could from the Kadorians, and one day, they'd take everything that they possibly could. Illary didn't know what would happen then, when the world was left as a wasteland. She supposed that the Alhmanics would leave, giving Kador back to the Kadorians with its irreversible pollution. Everyone would die, but the Alhmanics would be happy with the credits that they'd wrung from the dying Kadorians.

There was a loud strike on the enormous gong next to the altar, and the whole temple fell silent. The Mothers began chanting an ancient song of Alhmanic words that none of the Kadorians could understand. They sounded impressive, though, and what really mattered during the rituals was the showmanship, not the actual impact.

Father Alois began to pour the sacred water into Flower Shell Bowls, filling them with theoretically blessed water. Illary knew that the water was just plain water; it had no more power to heal than any other kind of water. He began to add his lower voice to the Mothers' chant, and shivers went down her spine. His voice was deep and resonant, and it overtook the Mothers' voices, though he was only one person and there were many Mothers.

She knelt beside Suyana. Father Aghi brought over some of the Flower Shell Bowls and set them in front of the sisters. With their hands linked, they spoke the words that their mother had taught them. They didn't sink actual power into this ritual — there was no point — so they drew on their illusion skills. The sparks of light always awed the bystanders and the Alhmanics alike, and it would be enough. Small sparks floated around the bowls.

Then the sacred water was passed around as everyone drank from the bowls. Illary felt sad that so many Kadorians were terminally ill from the pollution; they were beyond her healing skills now, and she hated watching people come day after day as they died by inches. It hurt her heart.

The Mothers, while still chanting, collected the bowls from the Kadorian faithful. The morning ritual was over when someone struck the gong a second time; the crowd dispersed. The Kadorians would go back to their day's work while the temple dwellers would clean the temple and make sure that it ran properly.

Illary saw Father Alois head in her direction while engaged in conversation with Father Aghi. She needed to get out of here.

Fast.

She grabbed Suyana's arm before quickly backing out of the main area of the temple. She wasn't paying attention to which door she pulled them through, so she was surprised to turn and see an entire ward of patients looking at the two of them. She tilted her chin up and kept walking, even as she saw that a Mother watching over the ward had narrowed her eyes at them. Illary needed to act like she belonged here.

She turned to Suyana, who was following her lead. It was important not to look guilty. They were running from their responsibilities, yes, but who could blame them?

At the end of the ward, they

could get into one of the hallways that went straight to the underground and overground stairwells, which led to locked exits to the outside. Illary stopped in that hallway, frozen by her choice. Would her telekinesis help her pick the locks? It wasn't very reliable.

Suyana moved past Illary, then she turned back.

"What are you doing? Do you want to be caught here, so close to the outside?"

Illary turned to her sister. "Let's

go. We should hurry."

Map

Illary

Illary and Suyana ran quickly when there was nobody to see them, straight back to their room. They had their normal rations, a roll of bread and cup of water each. It wasn't enough, not nearly enough, but it was all that they were permitted.

Suyana bit into her bread, taking a small bite to make it last longer. The girls had existed in a constant state of hunger since they entered the temple.

"Do you know what Qullqi told me?"

Illary sighed inwardly. Was Suyana going to become a big gossip like Qullqi? They had better things to do.

"What did Qullqi say?"

"She said that the Alhmanics were getting ready to crack down on Pachakutek's rebellion."

Illary looked at her sister sharply. "Crack down? How?"

Suyana just shook her head. "I have no idea. There are some plans to crush the rebellion; the Fathers haven't seen too much of it, but they're ready to kill anybody that they think might be involved or know anything about it."

Illary sighed. "There's not much that we can do. Eat your bread, Suyana."

Suyana and Illary finished their small meal, their stomachs still nearly empty afterwards.

Suyana yawned. "We didn't sleep

much last night."

"We didn't. Take a nap, Suyana."

Suyana lay down in their bed, still clad in her scratchy burlap clothing. They didn't know how long their reprieve would last, and they would need to be ready to go if anybody thought to look for them in their room.

Illary lay down next to Suyana; she could use some rest, too. Finally, when she heard Suyana's breathing change, she went to the heavy cloak that she used when the weather was chilly. Inside, she kept a very small scroll. The scroll would earn her a week or even a month of purification, but it held the key to her escape.

She rolled it out on the floor, tracing the lines of the route that would get them out of the heavily guarded temple and into the rebel sanctuary. Pachakutek knew that he could use Suyana and Illary's abilities as part of the rebel efforts; the hard part was getting to him.

She hadn't been outside of the temple in a long while, so Illary knew that she had to figure out how to get a map of the mountain range. The route was probably clear to someone who had traveled it, but it was as clear as mud for someone who had never seen it before.

She carefully rolled it back up and hid it again. She went to rest next to Suyana. Both of them were tired, and they might as well take advantage of this rare free time. She should be attending the sick at Father Alois' side, but she had escaped that fate, if only for a little while.

She closed her eyes and fell asleep.

Storm

Illary

Illary woke up to the sounds of an asteroid storm around them. There were many loud thumps as tiny bits of miniature asteroids fell around the temple. The temple was mostly sturdy, but the noise was quite scary. Illary could feel her heart thumping in her chest every time she heard a boom.

Illary was thankful for the storm.

Because of the storm, few if any Kadorians would come to be healed at the temple, which meant that she could continue to avoid Father Alois.

Maybe the storm was a sign...a sign that she should leave now while she was still untouched. Leaving was really her only option.

"Illary?"

Suyana's sleep-deepened voice made Illary turn around to see her little sister sitting up on the bed.

"It's just a storm, Suyana." She leaned down and kissed her little sister's cheek. They might be young women now, but she could never forget the tiny little girl that Suyana had once been, sucking on her thumb and carrying a filthy doll everywhere. Illary was only a little older than her, but as the middle child, she'd been expected to help with Suyana, especially when Kaley and their mother were out tending the sick.

Illary heard the curtain slide open as the circular metal rings rasped on the metal rod. She whipped around to see men in boots with silvery tags swinging from chains around their necks entering the room.

Illary felt her heart beat faster. Had Father Alois sent them to purify her?

After looking more closely at them, they had a logo on their coats that said "Kandalph Space Marines, Inc.". She had seen mercenaries in passing when she was younger, of course, but this was the closest that she'd ever gotten to one.

"We need to move now."

Who were these men who decided that they could order her around? Suyana put a trembling hand in the crook of Illary's elbow. Illary lifted her chin.

"Who are you?"

Just then, she heard an ominous creak coming from the ceiling. It seemed that the temple might not be able to withstand the storm after all. If the temple caved, they might be trapped inside.

On the other hand, these space

marines didn't seem trustworthy, bursting out of nowhere and ending up in their room.

"We'll find our own way out, thank you." Suyana and Illary got off the bed and moved towards the door.

After a split second, Illary found Suyana's hand torn away from her elbow. She was now upside down and over the shoulder of one of the space marines.

"Hey!" She hit the space marine who was carrying her over and over again, but he acted as if she was doing less than nothing. "Put us down!"

Glancing back at her room, she could see that there were still space marines inside of her room, gathering their things. It looked like they wouldn't be coming back to the temple.

Why were they being stolen?

"Put me down!" Illary demanded. They still acted as if she hadn't said anything at all. She was jostled as the space marines broke into a run, going straight for the hallways that would bring them outside. She heard several beeps when they got to the door, and she realized that somehow the KSM men had the codes to unlock the doors. They were with the Alhmanics.

Her heart rate sped up as she struggled to get out of the space marine's hold, but he kept a firm grip on her. She couldn't see Suyana now, but she couldn't scream her name without attracting attention; she didn't want Father Alois to come by and tell the space marines to put her into his care.

Then they were outside of the temple. Illary breathed in the air outside of the temple for the first time. It was tainted with the pollution that the Alhmanics had released; they kept expensive and energy-intensive purification systems inside of the temple. Still, Illary was glad to smell Kadorian earth again, if only for a little while.

Illary was finally put down and stuffed inside of an extremely small motorized vehicle. She was stuffed into a seat behind the driver's seat, and they were so close together that her legs were straddling the seat in front of her. Then the space marine who had carried her got into the vehicle and started it up.

The doors closed. Illary could now smell the scent of the space marine, a dark, masculine musk. She hadn't had much to do with men since she became a full-time healer, and she blushed because she suddenly had her legs around one in this tiny vehicle.

She noticed, now that she was no longer upside down, how broad his shoulders were. They were wider than the seat in front of her and about twice the width of Illary's own shoulders. No wonder he'd been able to pick her up as if she weighed no more than Suyana's old doll.

"Where are you taking me?"

"You'll see when we get there."

She knew that it was useless to ask more questions, so she stared out the front window, looking at the Kadorian city near the temple. It was dirty and in disrepair, since people could barely afford to feed themselves and stay alive. Repainting their signs fell very low on their list of priorities. Like her, many of the Kadorians were too thin.

Her heart ached when she thought of her people going hungry. The food supply of edible and non-toxic food was strictly controlled by the Alhmanics and carefully given to them on a ration system.

They quickly sped through town, heading towards the space docks where there were large ships. Illary hadn't spent much time around spaceships when she was younger; she marveled at how huge they were. They seemed to be as large as the temple. How could they be launched into space?

Scanners

Illary

The space marine got out of the vehicle and pulled Illary out. He kept a tight grip on her waist. She felt warmth spreading throughout her midsection. She'd never been touched like this. He smelled so good, and he was so close.

He was also the enemy. Illary stopped feeling like her insides were melting when she remembered that he'd stolen her from the temple right as she was about to escape and join Pachakutek's rebellion. Without Illary and Suyana, could they succeed? After years under their thumb, Illary wanted to expel the Alhmanics from Kador. She wouldn't shed a tear if Father Alois was killed in the uprising.

They went to the door of the ship, but then the space marine stopped.

"Wait."

He reached into his belt and pulled out some kind of wand.

"Stand still."

Illary froze in place as he came even closer to her. It was hard to think when he was this close, his face just inches from hers, his fresh breath tickling her nose.

"I need to check you for alien viruses."

"I'm not sick."

"I need to check you anyway."

He ran the wand all over her body. Illary could feel his warmth when he came close to her, and she couldn't believe how aware she felt of this strange space marine that she'd just met.

"I don't need to be scanned."

"Don't be afraid." He continued to wand her body. The wand beeped finally.

"All clear. You're disease-free, though slightly malnourished."

"Not a surprise," Illary replied. "I haven't been able to eat properly ever since they took me."

"Get inside."

Illary wanted to listen to him this time. She could always hope that they'd actually feed her, instead of controlling her by withholding food as the Fathers had. Doing any kind of health checkup meant that they cared about her well-being, didn't it? It wasn't just to make sure that she didn't infect them with an alien disease. She felt hope unfold in her chest, although she wondered if she was leaping into his arms before she really understood the situation.

She'd heard rumors, mostly from Qullqi, about KSM. They said that KSM's primary purpose was to abduct fertile women and deliver them to husbands on worlds where they valued them highly. Illary didn't want to be one of KSM's Brides. She was too headstrong to ever kowtow to any husband, and now that she was out of the temple, she'd die before she ever let anybody dictate how she would live her life. She had been planning on escaping with Suyana so that they could find Pachakutek and join him.

And the space marines had ruined absolutely everything.

"No. Thank you for rescuing me during the storm. I'm going to join the on-planet rebellion. Suyana," she called, "come on." They didn't have the map — she wasn't sure if the space marines who had taken their things had bothered to take Illary's cloak — but Illary was sure that if they got near Pachakutek's stronghold, someone would bring the two girls to the rebel leader. They were distinctive with their pure red hair, after all.

"You were retrieved under the

order of a family member."

"Prove it."

"I can."

The space marine slapped a panel on the outside of the spaceship. He marched into the opening. Illary looked through the door to see him use a retina scanner to boot up the ship. The screen flashed and then died.

The space marine walked to the screen and performed the age-old method of making technology work; he slapped it. It didn't help. The screen was still black.

He walked back to the doorway to tell Illary, "The storm must have caused some kind of malfunction. It might be a while before I can generate a report."

"I'm not coming with you until you can generate that report."

"Illary?"

Illary turned to see Suyana walking up to her while accompanied by another space marine. Suyana ran to her. Illary hugged her little sister, who was trembling from shock and uncertainty.

She closed her eyes and appreciated that her sister, for a few moments at least, was here, safe and sound. They were out of the temple, which was a major step forward. Illary had been Suyana's rock for all the years that Kaley had been gone. She couldn't fall apart now.

She didn't know if the space marine was telling the truth. He seemed okay, but her intuition wasn't finely honed. She hadn't been out of the temple in a long time, after all, and she wasn't the best at reading hidden intentions. Father Alois had been more than obvious when he'd asked her to learn naked rituals; any subtext that wasn't basically shouted could sometimes be lost on Illary.

Illary also didn't know if they had much of a choice. She was still outside of the ship, true, but the space marines had already demonstrated in Illary and Suyana's room that they would be happy to pick them up and move them wherever they wanted the sisters to go. What if they were being acquired as Brides for some men who wanted healer wives?

She didn't like that option, but she also didn't like the alternative. The Alhmanics had a huge number of guards, especially since they ruled a planet that they hadn't treated kindly. The Fathers and Mothers would never let Illary and Suyana, who pulled in a large amount of money for the temple, leave easily.

Suyana was crying silently now, and Illary patted her back and rubbed it in a circular motion. Leaning towards Suyana's ear, she hummed Suyana's lullaby, the one that their mother had always used when Suyana cried as a baby. She felt the tension in Suyana's body ease. Illary wished that she was as easy to calm; they could be duped into becoming Brides for KSM. Who knew what awaited them if that was the case?

"Come inside. We shouldn't stay on this planet for too long. The guards will trace us." The space marine who had stolen Illary was speaking to them. "You're too thin. You'll have enough food on our ship; we'll have our healer make sure you get proper nutrition."

The offer of enough food to fill their stomachs would be enough to lure them into the spaceship. If they were being sold as Brides, at least they wouldn't be hungry. Illary caught Suyana's eyes and nodded just a fraction of an inch.

They walked into the open doorway. The regiment of space

marines filtered into the ship, too. Illary and Suyana settled into a comfortable gel-padded couch with a few metal straps which automatically wrapped around them. They leaned back as the ship sputtered and lurched; finally, they heard the engines engage as they were propelled into space.

Overcome with exhaustion by everything that had happened, Illary felt herself falling asleep while Suyana slept on the couch beside her, the bonds of the couch holding them securely in place.

Dining Hall

Illary

Illary woke up when she felt a warm hand touch her shoulder. Her eyes went wide as she looked at the man standing over her. He was the space marine who had stolen her.

"Do you want to eat?"

"Yes."

She looked over at her little sister, who was still fast asleep. Suyana had always needed more rest than Illary; she didn't want to wake her, even for food.

"Come to the dining hall."

Illary slid off of the couch so that Suyana wouldn't hear her moving. She followed the space marine into a room that had shelves full of more food than she could ever eat. She felt her jaw drop at the extraordinary amount of food there. Maybe her idea of the cost of food was skewed since the Alhmanics imported a lot of food from off-world, but the food in this room cost an absolute fortune.

"Eat anything you like. Our nutritionist took a look at your initial scans while you were asleep. He said that you need to focus on getting certain key nutrients. You need to eat a lot of red meat, too. You're slightly anemic, and so is your sister."

"Believe me, you aren't going to have any trouble convincing us to eat." Illary bee-lined for something that looked like beef jerky. She tore open the package and pulled off a piece. She put it into her mouth and then immediately began to cough.

"Stars above, this is spicy!"

"It's kho bo cay from Dalat. Didn't you notice that it was covered with red pepper seeds?"

In her haste to eat some of the delicious food that they had stored in the ship, she hadn't bothered to look too closely at the beef jerky.

"It's pretty good...if you like having your mouth on fire."

"I'm pretty sure that the nutritionist would approve of drinking some milk. It'll help take away some of the burn."

He pulled open their cold storage, and Illary felt a blast of cold air coming out as he brought out a carton of milk. She didn't know what kind of milk it was; she wasn't going to ask. She was familiar enough with Kadorian animals, but she had no idea where KSM was based. She knew better than to ask what kind of alien animal had produced the milk; she didn't actually want to know.

He poured it into a tall glass. She chugged it down gratefully. The cool milk helped put out the fire in her mouth, and she ended up eating the whole package. Her stomach felt over-stuffed; she hadn't had so much meat in years, if ever. She crumpled the empty package in her hand and sighed, rubbing the slight ache from her stomach being so full.

"Done?"

She nodded.

"What's your name?"

The space marine laughed. "I guess that I haven't introduced myself yet. I'm sorry, I've been so focused on extracting you from Kador that I didn't realize that you haven't been studying my file as I've studied yours. I'm Xun."

"Illary, but you already know that."

"It's nice to meet you, Illary." He bowed to her, just a quick bowing of the head.

She didn't know why, but Illary trusted him for some reason. He was nice enough to her, at least for now, and he'd fed her. She could guard her heart, but Suyana, younger and a little more naive, would be easy prey for this kind of simple kindness. She'd have to watch Suyana before the KSM men were able to convince them to accept their inevitable fate as Brides.

"Xun, you said earlier that you had a report that could show me that a family member authorized the extraction. You haven't provided any proof at all why you've stolen us." She needed to protect Suyana and herself.

"Of course. If you're full for now, we should go back to the main area."

Illary tossed the empty package

into a waste receptacle before following him. Xun was at a large control panel tapping some buttons to move things around on the big screen. Obviously, the storm hadn't done any lasting damage; they must have repaired it while she slept.

Kaley's picture was on the screen now. Illary covered her gaping mouth with one hand. It was a picture of Kaley, an older Kaley. She looked happy and well fed.

"Kaley?"

"Yes. She's married to Prince

Jesaja. They sent us to fetch you from Kador."

"A prince? What?"

"He's the avatar of Tiwaz."

"What?"

"Intara's warrior god."

Okay, maybe they really weren't with the Alhmanics. According to Alhmanic doctrine, the only god in the stars was Ziu.

"Wait a minute, she's married? Already?"

Xun shrugged. He probably saw marriages happen constantly. For

Kaley, Suyana, and Illary, dating anybody had been the furthest thing from their minds; they'd just tried to survive and not cause any trouble.

"She's having a child."

Illary felt like the spaceship had suddenly dropped back into the atmosphere. Her stomach certainly felt like it, anyway. "What?" Too much information, too fast.

"Kaley is pregnant with Jesaja's heir."

"She's so young!" Illary protested.

"She's an adult. She can have

children if she wants."

Illary guessed that Xun was right.

Xun changed the subject. "Do you want to take a tour of the ship? We're pretty stable at the moment, and it would be a good idea for you to understand where you are."

Illary nodded. "That would be great."

Xun turned away from the control panel and brought her into the corridor.

"This is the room that controls

our cloaking system. It helps us hide in plain sight."

A cloaking system for the spaceship definitely made sense. They'd been able to extract them from the temple with a minimum amount of fuss. Yes, the storm had definitely helped, but surely one of the Alhmanic guards would have seen the large spaceship if they had cared to notice.

"And through this hallway is the holo-deck."

"What's this room for?"

"It's for recreation. You can play any number of games that you want or run different simulations." Illary didn't know what he meant by running simulations, but she didn't want to look stupid when she asked. She was quiet as Xun moved to the next room.

Clothes

Illary

"In here, we have a Fitter."

"Fitter?"

"It can measure you. We have a deluxe version that was custom-made for KSM, so it can make a number of pre-programmed outfits as well. We don't keep tailors on KSM ships; they're deadweight. The Fitter does all of our uniform repairs."

"Can I try it out?" She hadn't said

anything, but the burlap dress that she was wearing wasn't very comfortable.

"Of course."

Illary stepped into the Fitter. Xun pressed some kind of button that made the glass door close. He looked at her as she was scanned. When the Fitter was done, the door opened.

Illary stepped out and she was immediately confronted with the naked outline of her body. She felt her cheeks turn the color of her red hair.

"The Fitter makes clothes that are tailored specifically for you. Here, choose an outfit. There isn't a wide variety, since all of the clothes are KSM-issue, but it might be better than the burlap dress that you've been wearing."

He wasn't commenting on being able to see her body essentially naked, so she wouldn't comment, either.

"Just tap the outfit that you want."

She saw that there was a

touchscreen on the side of the Fitter. She pressed the arrows on each side, curious about what it would be able to do. The Alhmanics had much more advanced technology than the Kadorians, and they were careful to keep it away from them, just in case the Kadorians understood how to use it against them.

"Stop switching between screens. Just choose one outfit. Maybe two. You can always come back here later."

Illary chose a uniform that was

dark grey and blue.

"That's our marine world outfit. It's made out of scuba knit material...very sturdy, lightweight, and stretchy."

Illary could hear the machine whirring before she saw an outfit being dispensed at the side. She went to pick it up.

The KSM outfits that were programmed into the machine were meant for men, and it wasn't a very feminine outfit. But she had to admit that the material was far more comfortable than the burlap that she'd worn for years.

"If you'd like to change, I'll step out into the corridor."

"I'll just take a minute."

Xun nodded and walked outside, closing the door. Illary quickly shed the itchy burlap. If she could burn it, she would. She stepped into the scuba knit uniform, breathing a huge sigh of relief. It felt a lot better on her skin.

She almost felt like a new person with her new outfit. She looked longingly at the machine, ready to request more outfits, but she knew that Xun was waiting outside. She would bring Suyana back here when she woke up, and then they'd both be able to get as many outfits as they wanted from the pre-programmed patterns.

She went out into the corridor. Immediately, she could see a change in Xun's attitude. His eyes swept her up and down. His pupils dilated.

"You look...different."

Illary looked down at herself.

There weren't any mirrors in the room she'd just left. She noticed that the material followed the outline of her body exactly. Her generous curves were accentuated while the fabric came in at the waist to outline the narrowness of it.

She felt herself blushing.

"It's marvelous what new clothes can do," she said briskly, pretending as if it weren't the first new outfit she'd had beyond burlap dresses since being taken in by the Alhmanics.

Xun continued the tour, but Illary was lost in her own thoughts, unable to pay attention to the different parts of the ship. Her eyes followed the dark-eyed officer; when he'd looked at her body, she'd felt warmth in the pit of her stomach. She had never been in such close proximity to an attractive man before he'd stolen her and stuffed her into the vehicle that had brought her to the ship. Surrounded by the Fathers and Mothers inside of the Alhmanic temples with a few acolytes like

Qullqi, Illary had barely interacted with outsiders beyond healing them. She had dim memories from when she was young, of course, but they were faded. She didn't understand what Xun made her feel, and she couldn't pay attention while he was talking in that deep, velvety voice that made her feel like she was a cat and he was stroking her back.

Her reverie was interrupted by a loud, blaring alarm which made her jump.

Attack

Illary

"Battle stations," a robotic voice said. "Report to your battle stations."

The temple guard must have found them. Illary's stomach sank as she thought about being taken back to the temple. She would face the worst punishment ever.

"I'll take you to the safe room. Move."

He began to jog in the corridor.

Illary followed him as quickly as she could, then she remembered that her little sister was still asleep on the gel couch.

"Suyana!"

Illary turned around and began to run for Suyana, but Xun caught her arm and pulled her towards the safe room despite her struggles.

When they got to the safe room, Suyana was already there. Illary ran to hold her little sister, who was shaking even worse than she had been when they'd first been stolen.

In that moment, Illary was thrown off of her feet, landing in a heap on the floor as the ship rocked. Some kind of pulsar blast had hit them.

She looked at Xun, who was in a fighter's crouch on the ground.

"Stay calm. Wait here. I'll be back."

He left the safe room, sealing the door. She could hear some kind of mechanism engage. They'd be safe...for a little while anyway.

"I think that the temple guards

have found us, Illary."

"I think so, too. The ship is supposed to be cloaked, but they have enough money to afford technology to detect us." All of the money that the Fathers had made from Illary and Suyana's labor had been spent to fund the most sophisticated surveillance systems that money could buy. It wasn't surprising that they could see KSM's cloaked ship, even after they went off-planet.

With a horrible screech, the

metal of the safe room's door crumpled from some kind of blast. The sisters were horrified to find that their safe room had been breached by whatever weapons the Alhmanics were using. They obviously didn't care about taking them alive. They could've been killed.

"We've got to get out of here," Illary told her. "Let's go to the kitchen. Their cabinets are sturdy."

Suyana followed Illary through the half-destroyed door. Illary ran, one hand on the wall to keep her upright, as the ship rocked as blast after blast hit them.

"Hurry!" Illary called back to Suyana. She didn't know if they would make it. Her heart was thumping loudly as she ran and stumbled her way to the kitchen.

Then they were finally inside, and she opened pantry doors, throwing perfectly good food on the ground. Everything was packaged, so she hoped that it would be fine afterward. Right now, she and Suyana needed to take up that space.

They got inside of the same cabinet and hugged each other as the ship continued to rock around them. Illary felt a package beneath her, so she pulled it out and opened it. It smelled like fruit. She passed the open package to Suyana so that her little sister could eat something while they waited. Being permitted to eat anything they wanted was nearly nirvana for the two of them, and it was the silver lining of this frightening attack. Illary would wait here until the attack stopped, keeping Suyana safe and full.

Evacuation

Xun

When it became clear that the ship was going down — something was penetrating their defenses — Xun ran to the safe room. One of the engines was already dead, and the other one could only sustain about two more hits before going off-line as well.

With dismay, he realized that the door to the safe room had been destroyed. Heart pounding hard, he looked inside. Had the girls been hurt?

To his relief, there wasn't anybody in the room. But Xun had no idea where they were; they needed to evacuate the ship immediately, and they were nowhere to be seen.

"Illary!" Xun bellowed. Nobody answered.

"What's wrong?" Phuoc asked. He was in the same corridor.

"They're missing. The safe room was breached by one of the hits.

Something went wrong with the door. Can you help me find them?"

"Suyana!" Phuoc shouted. The shout echoed, but there wasn't any reply to Phuoc's call, either.

Phuoc and Xun made their way through the rest of the ship. They weren't in the corridors or the holo-deck. Suddenly, Xun remembered how happy Illary had been when they'd gotten food in the kitchen.

"Kitchen," Xun told Phuoc before beginning to run. He'd counted one more hit to the engine as they'd searched, and time was running out.

He hoped that they'd be able to find them before the ship began to free-fall into the vacuum of space without any hope of return.

When he got to the kitchen, he could see that there were unopened packages of food scattered on the ground. They had definitely come to the kitchen. He saw that everything was from the dried fruit compartment. He quickly walked around the packages on the ground to yank the cabinet open.

"We have to evacuate the ship right now."

The girls came out of the pantry. Xun and Phuoc brought them to the evacuation pods. Most of the KSM ships went without them due to their special permit, but this particular ship could take them due to its spacious size, which was lucky. The small evacuation pods would save their lives today.

"Get in," Phuoc said to Suyana. She went into the nearest pod before Phuoc joined her.

"Wait a minute! I don't want to be separated from Suyana."

"You don't have a choice. There are only two slots inside of the evacuation pods and you have no clue how to pilot one. You need to get in another one so that we can meet at the nearest space station. You need to trust us. We don't have any time to waste. We've waited too long as it is in order to find you two."

Illary looked at him. He could see it in her face when she made her decision, and he held back a sigh of relief when she walked to the other pod. The rest of their regiment had already bailed; the only people left on this priceless piece of junk were the four of them. He ducked into the pod after Illary and sealed it before pressing the button which would push them out of the ship and into the cold emptiness of space.

Bubble Suit

Illary

Metal straps twisted around
Illary to hold her in place as the pod
was ejected. She stayed in place while
the pod began its course to safety.
Her heart ached for her little sister.
They'd never been separated like this
before; they'd been together in the
temple for a very long time. Suyana's
absence made her fret about her
safety, but there wasn't anything that

Illary could do.

The metal straps retracted as the pod stabilized.

"Quickly. I need you to put on a bubble suit," Xun said.

"Bubble suit?"

"It will help you hover-step and keep your oxygen levels where they need to be. It's too small to show up on any radar. It also has a cloaking mechanism, which is far more effective for something small."

The bubble suit was very strange for Illary. She'd worn very few kinds of clothing over the past several years, and now she was wearing all kinds of different things. She struggled with the straps of the suit, which attached over the center of her chest. Try as she might, she couldn't get them on.

Xun, predictably, had his suit on in about a half second. After he watched her struggle with hers, he came forward and said, "Let me help."

Illary's hands dropped to her sides. She watched as Xun expertly twisted and clicked everything that needed to be put into place. When he was this close, she could smell his masculine scent strongly. Her nostrils flared, although she tried to hide her reaction. She couldn't get involved with anybody, and she'd never had any experience with men. A space marine would eat her alive.

The evacuation pod rocked right after her bubble suit was totally closed.

"We just took a hit. We'll have to hover-step to the station. Come on." He hit the button that had previously sealed the evacuation pod. Now it opened it up, letting them go straight into space.

He linked his arm with hers as he took huge, exaggerated steps in space. He wasn't walking on anything, but something in the suit was helping propel him forward. She was being dragged along with him, but she was pulling him back. She began to hover-step as he was stepping. Her heart was in her throat. If she messed up in space, she would die as soon as her oxygen ran out.

She had to admit that — life-threatening danger aside — it was pretty fun to space-walk inside of the bubble suit. She'd never hover-stepped before, but beyond needing to escape from the Alhmanic attack, she was definitely enjoying herself. Yes, her oxygen levels were getting lower by the second, making breathing a wee bit hard, but she felt safe with Xun beside her.

And then they came very close to a small satellite station. Illary was gasping now, her body fighting for air, and she knew that she didn't have much time left. She knew that panicking would use up all of her oxygen, though, so it would be counterproductive.

She watched as Xun keyed in a code to an outside lock. The door opened, and they were finally inside of the station. As soon as Xun closed the door to the outside, he moved quickly to a second door and keyed in another code to open it. Illary followed him into the interior of the small satellite station. Once they were both inside, he shut the second door and opened the helmet of his suit and breathed deeply. Illary followed his cue and took in a deep breath of oxygen-rich air, feeling it fill her lungs.

Space Dock

Illary

"Let's see what kind of vehicles we can find here."

He pointed towards a door and the two of them went towards it. When they went through it, Illary could see a wide variety of vehicles.

"This is one of the small stations that KSM has a contract with. I can take whatever I need and it'll go on this mission's bill. I hope your sister is fine with paying for our survival."

"She will be," Illary said instantly, although she had no clue what kind of financial situation her sister was in. Kaley would pay any price for her, she knew, and she'd help repay the debt in any way that she could once she was safe and reunited with her family members.

"Where's Suyana?" Illary said, looking around. "I thought that you said that we'd meet them at the station."

"No, this station is an unplanned

stop. Not to worry, though; we can find your sister later. Phuoc is with her, and he's one of the most skilled and honorable warriors inside of my regiment. You have nothing to worry about."

Xun turned and began to stop by each vehicle, waving his hand to make the technical specifications appear in a hologram next to each spaceship. He kept going, doing it for ship after ship.

Illary shifted from foot to foot, anxious about being inside of the satellite station alone with Xun. He could do anything he liked to her at the moment and nobody would know. If he wanted to kill her, she'd die. She had no self-defense training at all. The only reason she was alive was because of Xun's duty to KSM to deliver her on time. She felt exposed and a little scared, more so than when she'd been outside in the vacuum of space with only a bubble suit. He'd felt like her protector then, but now she had no clue what he was doing.

"What are you looking for?"

"A craft that can be handled by a single pilot." Xun turned to look at Illary. "Unless you have experience piloting a ship?"

"No," Illary said, shaking her head. "I've never done it."

"Then I'll keep looking. Most of these ships are too big to be handled by a single person."

Illary watched as he visited ship after ship. Then, finally, Xun stopped at a spaceship near the end of the line.

"This one is it."

She looked at it. It looked barely bigger than their emergency pod, although it would be slightly more comfortable.

"What is that?"

"It's a hover floater. It doesn't take much to steer it, but it's pretty small. I need you to come with me to their pantry and grab some meal packs. There isn't much on this ship."

Xun walked out of the space dock and into a corridor. Illary hurried after him; she was absolutely lost inside of this station, but he seemed to know what he was doing.

They came into a kitchen which was stuffed with food, just like the kitchen on the destroyed spaceship that they'd been forced to abandon. Illary filled her arms with food and Xun did the same. Then they walked back to the hover floater, careful not to drop any of their food packages.

Hover Floater

Illary

When they were inside of the hover floater, Xun bent to take out a rectangular metal box. He dumped the meal packets in his arms into it, then he pulled food packages from Illary's arms and put them in the box, too. Illary stood there, looking at the abundance of food. It was more food than she was permitted to eat in a week, although she didn't know just how much Xun needed.

"Hold out your arms."

"What?"

"I need to scan you to make sure that you aren't space sick. If my file is right, you've barely left the temple on Kador for many years."

"It's true, but I'm not space sick."

"I'm going to check."

Illary held out her arms so that Xun could wand her body again, moving into her personal space.

"Your heart rate is elevated, but other than that, you're fine." He gave her a brief smile before he turned to the controls and began the launch sequence.

She didn't know how to tell him that her elevated heart rate had nothing to do with space and everything to do with his proximity. When he was this close, she could feel the heat of his body touching hers. He was like a furnace.

She felt a lurch as the vehicle undocked and headed towards the door which was slowly sliding open. It was an airlock not unlike the one that they'd been through when they initially entered the station, but it was much larger in order to accommodate the size of the vehicles that would pass through it.

Then the outer door was open, and the hover floater moved into the dark space beyond the station. Illary was nervous enough to check the oxygen reading from a display that was glowing on one of the walls of the ship. She was reassured to see that the oxygen tanks were nearly full; they could last for a long time inside of the hover floater.

Unlike the other ships, there weren't any metal straps that automatically twisted around them in the hover floater. Illary found herself floating a little bit. Xun looked calm, though, and she guessed that the loss of pressure was expected. They floated upwards, coming close to one another. Illary struggled to grab hold of something, anything, and the closest thing was Xun. She held him to her, and their faces came close until less than an inch of space was between them. Overcome by feelings she didn't understand, Illary felt her whole body flush with heat when she was in such close proximity to her guard. She didn't know if her attraction to him was right or wrong, only that she felt very drawn to him. She knew that she was grateful for being rescued and delivered to her sister—it could just be gratitude. But her heart knew that there was something more than that.

The moment passed as the cabin's pressure increased enough for

Illary to stand on her own feet. Xun didn't look affected at all by their near-kiss. He bent towards the metal box where they'd deposited their food when they entered the ship.

"Now that we're on our way, let's eat."

Xun pulled out two meal packets from the rectangular metal box, pausing as he realized what Illary had taken from the kitchen.

"I took meal packets. You took snacks. You haven't done this before, have you?"

Illary blushed. "No. I've never been off-planet before."

Xun grunted before putting the meal packets into a machine. The machine hummed for a little bit, and Illary could hear running water. Then the machine dinged. Xun opened a panel to display steaming hot food perfectly presented on two immaculate white plates.

Illary's jaw dropped. She'd never seen technology like this. If the Alhmanics had it, they didn't use it on Kador.

"That food machine is amazing!"

"It's just a rehydrator, not a replicator," Xun said. "Do they not have these on Kador?"

"No." If they had, maybe Illary could have smuggled some food into her room and kept it out of sight without needing to endanger the kitchen staff.

He pulled out utensils to eat their newly rehydrated food and brought it to a small countertop that was against a wall, and then they ate in silence, Illary barely able to comprehend her good fortune. It seemed that he had no problem feeding her. She had years of malnourishment to fix. Maybe the damage was permanent, but she could try to eat as much nutritious food as she could.

As they finished their meal, the hover floater tilted a little bit.

Illary could feel her heart rate increase. "Are we being attacked again?"

Xun sprang to his feet and checked the control panel.

"No, there's just some astral wind here. I'll need to monitor the ship while we go through this tricky part."

Illary cleared away the plates that they'd used for food. There was a big sign that said DISPOSAL, and she put the plates in there and hoped for the best. She wasn't very familiar with spaceships, and she got the impression that KSM spaceships might be even more advanced than the kind that she'd seen as a child.

Illary walked around the hover floater because she had nothing to do. She pulled out drawers and opened cabinets; she had an insatiable curiosity, and it wasn't as if she could go into the holo-room that the big ship had had. She found small things tucked away in the corners of some of the compartments. Inside of a drawer, she saw a very small shiny rock, maybe a zirconia. It wasn't expensive, probably, but she liked it. Along with finding the rock, she found a very small golden ring hidden at the bottom of a cabinet. She was treasure-hunting on this little hover floater; she had to admit that her childhood innocence had been stolen from her when she was imprisoned and tightly controlled by the Alhmanics. She felt like a child on a scavenger hunt, before escaping, her life had all the fun sucked out of it by the Fathers and Mothers inside of the temple.

She would give the golden ring to Suyana, so she kept it safe in a pocket of her uniform. Their separation troubled her heart; it was all that she could do to quell her anxiety. She wanted to find Suyana and keep her close. She had to push aside the strange feelings that Xun inspired. She didn't have time to get involved with him, not if she wanted to make sure that her little sister was safe.

"We're almost there," she heard Xun say.

Convention

Xun

Xun stared at the space station on the screen. He had contacted the head of the space dock, and it seemed unusually full, though there would always be space for any KSM employee. The hover floater was programmed to get into their single empty space.

He hoped that they would be safe here at a large space station, where they couldn't be attacked without attracting attention.

"We're almost back to your sister, Illary."

"Good." Illary was hugging herself, and Xun wished that he could comfort her. He could see that she was worried, but he didn't know her well enough to hug her. He'd like to get to know her better, but this mission was too brief for them to really get closer.

"Phuoc should be there. If he's not, I'll go through the KSM communication channels and try to figure out his location."

The outside door of the station was opening now, and the hover floater easily made its way through the airlock and to the dock. Xun and Illary felt it when the hover floater attached itself to the dock.

"Let's go inside and see what we can find."

They got out of the hover floater and went into the station. KSM employees weren't asked questions, so they didn't have to deal with the dock master. They were unimpeded by regulations.

As soon as they entered the common area of the space station, they saw that hundreds of sentient beings were walking around. A giant banner said, "Welcome to Universal Health Co.!"

The administrators of the space station must have pulled out all the stops for the convention, because it was packed wall to wall. Xun could smell the scent of roasting meat; though he and Illary had recently eaten, the smell made his mouth water. He'd never turn down some roasted chicken or beef. During training, he regularly consumed all the protein he could find.

They passed several conference rooms which held even more people. He could see passionate speakers gesticulating and pointing towards the holograms of their presentations. It seemed that healers really cared about whatever they were meeting about. He thought that he saw the words "focused ultrasound", but he couldn't be sure. He wasn't all that familiar with medical terminology.

"Our first order of business is finding somewhere to stay. I need to make contact with my superiors and find Phuoc and Suyana. My regiment is floating somewhere out there in space."

"Sounds like a plan."

Xun looked around until he saw a sign that said LODGINGS. He put his arm around Illary's waist, feeling how soft she was, and pulled her in the direction of the lodgings.

Suite

Xun

Xun walked straight to the desk, bypassing the line of various species who were waiting for their turn.

"Hey!" a man shouted indignantly. "Take your place in line."

Xun turned around, touched the KSM logo on his uniform, and turned back. He heard Illary gulp. She probably didn't understand the power of the KSM name, but she'd just seen the slightest glimpse of it.

"How can I help you, sir?" The receptionist was looking at the KSM logo now.

"I'd like two rooms, please." No need to be rude. He'd probably used up whatever power he had when he'd cut in front of all these people.

"I'm sorry, sir. We only have one vacant room at the moment. It has a double bed, though."

"Unacceptable," he said crisply. He wasn't going to share a bed with the curvy and extremely beautiful

Kadorian that he was bringing back to her sister, who was a royal. Close proximity spelled disaster, and they'd already spent too much time in each other's company.

"Sir, I'm very sorry, but we can't kick anybody out. With the convention going on, it's impossible to get two rooms on very short notice. The only room that we have available is our presidential suite, reserved for visiting dignitaries. It's the best we've got."

Xun hoped that their presidential

suite had more than one place that could serve as a bed. He didn't want to spend a night with the tempting woman who smelled a little bit too delicious for her own good.

"Key, please."

She pulled out a radio key and put it into his hand.

"Shall I charge it to KSM?"

"Yes."

The key had a room number on it. He turned and motioned with his head for Illary to follow him to the elevators without saying another word to the receptionist.

They both got into an elevator with a Jalan warrior who had blue skin. Illary's eyes were wide, as if she'd never seen someone with blue skin before. She had a lot to learn, then. Jalan warriors were renowned in unarmed combat; it was their specialty. He'd have to see if any fights were scheduled. He was trained in unarmed combat, of course, but Jalans reportedly had moves that they never taught to anybody else. He might have an opportunity to pick up some new techniques.

The elevator stopped at their floor, and they got off. They walked through the corridor. Xun saw the room with the number that matched the key fob and scanned the radio key. The door opened for them and the two of them went inside.

In an instant, Xun's hopes about a second place to sleep were dashed. It had a bunch of small, delicate metal chairs. He didn't know if he could sit, let alone sleep on one. He'd never ask Illary to sleep on a metal chair, either.

Tonight was going to be pure torture.

Distraction

Xun

Xun was relieved to see a terminal sitting in the corner of the room. While he didn't like using unsecured technology to contact KSM, he didn't have a choice. He'd just have to make sure that he kept to the open lines.

He keyed a code into the terminal that would ring the glow-pad of the receptionist who his regiment routed everything through.

"KSM." He could see her hologram projected instantly into the room. She had dark grey hair and a terrifyingly intimidating manner. All of the space marines learned to respect her very quickly early on; if they didn't, she'd make sure that they were sent on the worst missions. Receptionists sometimes had an enormous amount of power, and she was one of them. She had been with KSM for an eternity, and nobody dared to offend her.

"Hello, ma'am," Xun said respectfully. "I'd like to log a request for two seats back to Intara from the space station that I'm calling from." He knew that she could trace his call. She probably had better tech skills than half of his regiment. "I need to report that I have Illary in custody, but Suyana is with Phuoc."

"Yes, we're aware that Suyana is with Phuoc. They're already on a spaceship back to Intara to reunite with Queen Kaley and God-King Jesaja." She tapped a few keys and frowned. "The next ship will dock for passengers tomorrow afternoon. That's the earliest I can move you."

"There aren't any ships that we can pilot back ourselves?"

"None are large enough; the reason why you were sent out with a large ship to begin with was the long journey."

Xun suppressed a sigh. "Thank you for your time."

"I'll send your travel information to this terminal. We'll see you soon, soldier." With a quick beep, her hologram disappeared.

Xun turned and saw that Illary was curled into a ball on the bed. She was hugging a pillow and crying gently.

He felt a spike of alarm. He came to sit on the bed beside her and stroked her back. "Hey. No need to cry." He could feel the edges of his mouth turning downwards. "You're okay."

"I wanted to see Suyana," she whispered. "We've never, ever been separated like this. I thought that

Phuoc and Suyana would be here to meet us and everything would be fine. But it's going to be another day before I can even get on a ship to Intara." Her tears were dripping onto her pillow and making a little puddle of tears.

Xun never liked seeing any female cry. He didn't want to sit in this room and watch her crying miserably.

"Why don't we go out there and see if there are any entertainment options?" He needed to distract her;

he couldn't fix their problems, but he could get her mind off of missing her little sister.

She wiped her eyes with the back of her hand. "Okay," she said in a husky tone that tugged at his heartstrings. He'd easily give up all of the pay from this mission if he never had to watch her cry again. Something inside of his heart said that she was the one for him, but he knew that he had to ignore that voice. She was the sister of a queen, and he was a young space marine. It would never work.

Recreation

Xun

Xun tapped on the terminal to find what kind of events that they had going on outside of the health convention. There was a live poetry reading, which he had no interest in, and a Jalan warrior duel.

"There's a Jalan warrior fight going on tonight. Would you like to go?"

"I've never really seen a lot of

fights," Illary said, her finger twirling in her hair. "Is it interesting?"

"You'll never know if you don't try." Xun tapped a few buttons. "We'll go down there and see if it's interesting. If it's not, we can do something else."

Xun knew that the fight ticket information would be connected to their radio key fob, since he'd charged it to the hotel room. He went to the door and held it open for Illary. Her eyes were still red from crying, and he wished that he could change that.

They walked towards the big amphitheater inside of the station. It was about half-full. It seemed that healers like violence, but not as much as the next person. They probably didn't love it since they were the ones who had to stitch people back together.

A bell rang loudly as the referee started the match. The two fighters circled each other, fists up. They wore no protective gear or pads. Their fight was full-contact.

Xun could feel his heart rate pick up. He'd been taught to fight, of course, but he'd been taught to fight inside of KSM, which took reasonable safety measures most of the time. This bare-fisted, unprotected fight was something else. He paid attention to the footwork of the Jalan warriors; it was very strange and unlike anything he'd ever seen before. They were doing something with their feet that made it look like they were engaging in a very fast dance, skittering away from each other as one of them got close. They were circling each other, waiting for an opening.

Xun longed to get in a physical fight, a contest of strength like the one below, but he knew that he could not. The fighting caused long-term brain damage, and it would not help his career at KSM at all. There were annual check-ups to ensure that they were still in fighting shape. If they weren't, they'd be fired immediately. KSM hired the best and focused on keeping only the best.

He turned to see Illary leaning her chin on her closed fist.

"Is this interesting?"

Illary shrugged. "I've never really watched anyone fight."

He could tell from her tone that she wasn't anywhere near as thrilled as he was to study their fighting techniques.

"Let's go."

"But you're really enjoying it."

"I can watch fights any day. But my time with you is limited."

She was quiet after he reminded

her that their sojourn together was a brief moment.

"How do you feel about poetry?"

He saw her face brighten.

"I love poetry. I write it whenever I can."

He suppressed a groan. He hated poetry.

Storytime

Xun

They went out and quickly paid for entry to the poetry reading.

To his surprise, Xun didn't hate it. Everyone had some kind of VR goggles that made the words come to life...almost literally. As they heard the poet speak in front of them, they could literally see the action going on.

The poet finished a story...something about a rabbit

hopping around in a garden...before the crowd burst into applause.

"My next story is for adults only. If there are any children in the room, they need to leave now."

The room filled with the sound of laughter. Because of the convention, every possible spot was taken by a healer. There weren't any children in the audience.

"My tale comes to us from Releon, a planet full of stories. Listen and watch."

Xun could hear the crowd quiet.

The poet must be a good storyteller.

"Long ago, arranged marriages were common on some planets. This story is from Releon."

Xun quietly snorted. Only two generations ago, his own grandparents had been part of a dynastic marriage to wed one wealthy and well-established family with strong Zhongguo roots with a newer, but even wealthier family that had made a fortune by finding the most innovative health technology in the universe and bringing it to planets where people would pay the most. Dying people would pay almost any price to stay alive, and his grandmother's family had profited handsomely by saving lives. His grandmother's family would have highly preferred for him to become a healer, but he'd never been patient enough to do it.

He respected the fact that Illary had put up with it for so long, imprisoned though she'd been.

"A young healer was told to marry a fearsome warrior king. She would bring peace to his kingdom by tending his sick heir, the son of his first wife who had died in childbirth. The king's cousins were eagerly waiting for the heir to die so that they could take his spot. But the king loved his child, and he would do anything to find a cure."

"So he searched his entire planet — this was before the Releons understood interplanetary travel — and found that there was a family of healers rumored to be able to cure anything, even death. He asked for

the daughter's hand in marriage,
sight unseen. If she was able to cure
his son, then he'd be happy. If she
wasn't, then he wouldn't mind
remaining married to her. She was
rumored to have unbelievable
beauty."

"Her family was overjoyed at their
beautiful daughter's good fortune.
But the daughter herself wasn't quite
so happy. The night before she was to
begin her journey to wed the strange
king, she ran away from her family's
home and took to the forest."

"There, she hid inside of a cave and waited for time to pass. After all, if he could find another healer or bring his son to her family, the child would be healed and all would be well."

"What she didn't know is that her family would refuse to heal the child until she had wed the king. They were all fully capable of it, but they were angry that their daughter had thrown away this chance. The king was not their king, and though he ranted and raved, he could not force them to heal his sick child."

"Every day, he watched the child get closer to death, inch by inch."

"One night, the king had a vision of a maiden living in a forest in a cave underneath a waterfall. He was taken by her pure beauty; she was decorated in rainbows from the light refracting through the waterfall."

A beautiful maiden who was decorated in rainbows? That sounded like Illary.

"He was betrothed to an absent healer, true, but he couldn't get the image of the rainbow woman out of his mind. So he set out to find waterfalls like the one in his dream. While he couldn't find the healer, perhaps he could find the mysterious rainbow woman."

"It was easy enough to find the waterfall where the cave might be. It was in the kingdom where he was staying, the kingdom of the healer bride."

"When he understood where it was, he set off by himself to meet the mysterious woman. When he came to the waterfall, he hid to the side and saw her pass through the waterfall."

"She was soaked to the skin by the spray, but she didn't seem to care. It was almost as if she were a water spirit. He could see that birds flew behind the waterfall to be tended by her. They would flap as they got in with an unsteady flight and come out stronger than before."

"He came in closer to hear her singing to the birds. Something in her voice was making them stronger."

"He had intended to marry a

young healer for her abilities, but maybe the rainbow woman could heal his son. Growing bold, he went through the waterfall to meet the woman who haunted his dreams."

"As soon as she saw him come through the waterfall, she ran deep into the cave. He followed her, only to find a labyrinth waiting there. She had chosen her hiding place well."

"He turned around before he could get lost in the darkness. Surprise had obviously not worked. How could the king convince the healer to speak to him?"

"That night, when he was starting the fire at his small camp, he had an idea. He put his hand in the flame. He, too, would be a wounded bird."

"Wincing from the terrible pain, he walked to the waterfall. From his earlier vantage point, he could see that she was back at the cave entrance, tending more small animals."

"'Help,' he called. 'Please help.'"

"He walked towards the waterfall

again, but this time he waited
outside. In a few moments, she stuck
her head out and looked at him. He
showed her his burnt hand."

"'Can you heal me?'"

"She hesitated, but then she told
him, 'Come in.'"

"So he came behind the waterfall
with her. She sang softly to his hand,
words that cooled his heated skin like
pure ice, but he wasn't frozen. He
watched in amazement as his skin
became pink and healthy under her
touch. A woman with this kind of

power would definitely be able to cure his son."

"'Please come back with me,' the king begged. 'My son is terminally ill.'"

"The woman bit her lip. 'I cannot. I'm hiding from my betrothed, you see. I can't leave this cave.'"

"'I will offer you money and jewels beyond imagining,' the king promised, 'if you'll only heal my son.'"

"'I have no interest in money or jewels.'"

Xun guessed that this king was

about to be very disappointed.

"'What can I offer you? I'll give you anything you like.'"

"'First, I would like freedom. Second, I'd like to set up a hospital to heal anybody who comes. Third, I would like some help in finding love. I have no wish to be sold off like chattel.'"

Three conditions were traditional in a lot of stories; this story sounded like a fairy tale from Zhongguo, and Xun felt the story distract him from his cares and bring him back to his nursery school days.

"'I can give you all of those things,' the king replied. 'Will you come with me?'" Rising to her feet, she extended her hand to the king, who raised it to his lips to kiss it and seal their bargain.

"She traveled with him out of the forest, back to the horse that would bring them to his kingdom. She visited his sick son, and with a single song, she healed the child."

"The king was overjoyed that she had kept her side of the bargain, so he kept his. First, he gave her an army to protect her and go wherever she wished. Second, he gave her a hospital near the palace. Third, he began a large tournament so that she could marry whichever warrior she wished."

"She began a contest. Many of the warriors who came expected a show of arms, but she tested them in languages, medicine, diplomacy, and manners. At the end of the tournament, not a single warrior had passed all of her tests."

"'I cannot help you any further in your quest for love,' the king told her sadly. 'I fear that you have rejected every possible candidate.'"

"'There is one other,' the young healer told him. 'Would you be my lover?'"

"The king didn't know what to say to the young healer. She was young, and he was much older than she was. But his heart had been empty since his first wife, his first queen, had died, and his people would love to have a new queen on the throne. His wife had made him a better person, and he knew that the healer would, too."

"'Yes,' he said. He arranged for a lavish wedding to take place inside of the palace. He gave her anything she desired. She didn't want a fancy party, just a large one with as many of his subjects as they could handle. The food that they ate was simple but filling, and everyone danced until the musicians gave up."

"That night, their wedding night, the king took the new queen to his chamber to sleep with her in his bed. But he found himself, though he'd sired a son, strangely shy. The new queen had an ethereal beauty and freshness that he'd lost long ago, if he'd ever had it."

"He found himself shy about his body in a way that he hadn't been since he was a young boy with a growing body. But his new wife was naked as soon as they went into their room. She came to him with all the fiery passion of youth, and he fell deeply in love with her that night. His love for her had been gentle; he knew that their marriage would last. But when she consumed him with the fire of her passion, his heart healed as he listened to the cries of her orgasm, the sweetest song that he had ever heard."

Xun's cheeks were warm now as he watched the king and his new bride make love through the VR goggles. He adjusted his pants a little. He hoped that Illary was as caught up in the story as he was.

"Of course, the young healer that

he had found behind the waterfall was his betrothed. She sent a letter to her parents, who traveled to the king's nearby kingdom. They apologized for withholding their help before; he forgave them, because without their refusal, he'd never have found the rainbow queen. And they lived happily ever after."

Xun joined the applause this time as he watched the queen kiss the king and present him with a new baby. Something inside of Xun's chest ached. He needed to focus on his career inside of KSM at the moment, but he knew that he wanted a family one day. There was a universe-wide shortage of fertile females, but he hoped that he'd be able to find a soulmate one day, one that he wouldn't have to pay to acquire.

"Thank you all." Xun took his goggles off in time to see the poet leave the stage. Illary was taking her goggles off too, and putting them into a bin at the side of the room. Xun quickly threw his goggles into the receptacle before moving towards the doorway, one hand on Illary's waist.

"Let's go back to our room."

Spätburgunder

Illary

Xun brought her towards their hotel room. She liked being out and about after her time confined in the temple, but she had to admit that she was experiencing just a little agoraphobia. She'd been in large crowds before, of course, but never like this. As a healer, she'd always been set aside during a ritual, not immersed in a sea of people. They were soon back to their hotel suite.

"I'm so thirsty," Illary told Xun. "Is there anything to drink?"

"Why don't we order food? I could do with a meal."

"Sounds good to me." There was a part of the terminal where they could order hand-prepared food. Xun ordered something, and it was at their hotel room door on a hover-trolley within 2 minutes. They must have very advanced robots inside of the station.

Illary pulled the hover-trolley to

the suite's small table. She brought the plates to the table and brought the utensils from the hover-trolley, too. Xun and Illary sat down to eat a generous meal that smelled just divine. There were carrots, slivers of chicken breast, and a whole lot of egg noodles with chopped mushrooms and bean sprouts mixed in. It wasn't a particularly intricate dish, but it tasted very good. The broth had a spicy aftertaste to it that made Illary's mouth tingle.

"What is this?"

"It's a Yuenanren dish called mi ga. The name just means egg noodles and chicken, but the language of Dalat is definitely a very literal one."

"Do you speak it?"

"I've picked up some of it. I trained on the base that was set up on Dalat, so it would be hard not to pick up some local flavor."

Illary nodded. "Dalat sounds like an interesting place. I still feel kind of hungry, though. I drank my soup, but I'm still thirsty." Illary turned to look at the small cooling cabinet inside of their room. "Maybe there are some drinks in there."

Illary opened the cooling cabinet. Inside, there were dozens of bottles.

"What's ruou?"

"It's a very strong alcohol from Dalat. Do you drink much?"

Illary cocked her head in puzzlement. "No."

"Then don't drink it. How about some nice wine?"

"Sounds good to me." Illary had only had ceremonial wine during certain rituals, so she didn't want to start with strong liquor.

Xun took a bottle of wine out of the cooling cabinet and put the bottle into a slot on the door. Instantly, a robotic arm uncorked the wine.

"Hundreds of years of technology just to learn that wine is best kept with a cork in it. We drink it just like the ancients." He poured the wine into glasses from a cabinet beside the cooling cabinet, then he gave one to her.

"Cheers." He held up his glass.

Illary raised her glass, mimicking

his gesture, and then drank her first sip of non-sacramental wine.

"Wow, this is really nice." She gulped down her wine much faster than Xun, who was slowly sipping his.

"More, please."

"Pace yourself. You aren't used to drinking too much alcohol."

"I'll be fine." The alcohol was starting to have a nice effect on her, making her feel warm. She could feel her cheeks heating a little bit. She smiled and leaned back in her chair.

"What kind of wine is this?"

"It's Intaran spätburgunder."

"It smells good…tastes good. More, please."

"I'm cutting you off after this glass. It's not a good idea for you to drink too much."

Illary flapped her hand at him and finished off a third glass.

"Whoa! Why is the room spinning?" She felt as if she were floating in space again. She took an experimental step forward; like hover-stepping, she fell a little bit with each step.

"You've had too much just a little too fast. Hold on, let's put you to bed."

Illary felt Xun lift her out of her chair and bring her to a bed. An idea struck her as he bent to lay her down, and she pulled the collar of his uniform, kissing him lightly on the lips when their faces were close enough.

He sprang back as quickly as if he had touched a flame.

"No. You're inebriated. Bad idea."

Illary stuck out her lower lip. "But you're handsome, and we're alone in a bedroom together. Didn't the story affect you at all?"

"It's the alcohol talking, Illary. Just close your eyes and go to sleep. If you still feel that way in the morning, we'll consider it."

Illary yawned. The alcohol was making her sleepy as well as uninhibited.

"Okay." She felt herself fall asleep.

Breaking the Rules

Xun

Xun woke up to find Illary's hand on his cock. In an instant, the events of the night before came rushing back.

"Good morning," she told him. "I've slept off the wine. I might have needed it to be brave enough to ask you for this, but I want to follow through on it." She stroked his cock again, making him moan.

"Ah!" he said, his hips shifting.

He watched in wonder as Illary's mouth came down on his cock.

"Have you done this before?"

"Never."

But somehow her tongue knew just how to pleasure him, and he hissed in a breath as he found himself rising towards a peak.

He didn't know what nano-bots did when they were released inside of a female's mouth, but he wasn't about to find out. He pulled her head off of his rod and pushed her on her back. Her red hair spilled around her, and looking at her now, right under him, she was the most beautiful sight that he had ever seen. Her curves were lush, and he bent to kiss them, taking her nipples into his mouth in turn. She arched her back beneath him, and he knew that she was ready.

He took his hard rod and put it between her thighs, resting the head of his cock against her for a minute before pushing inside. He felt something that surprised him.

"Virgin?"

She nodded, her eyes tightly closed. "Don't stop."

He pushed in a little harder, past her barrier. She hissed in a breath, then she let it out slowly.

"Mm. Good."

He took that as his cue to start moving inside of her, pushing himself deeper and deeper inside of her welcoming body. She was moaning now. He pulled her legs over his shoulders as he watched her mouth open before she climaxed beneath him. Her muscles milked him.

Then he felt his seed pouring into her and the nano-bots releasing inside of her. He was still hard, despite having just come, so he went for a second climax. He put his hand on her clitoris in order to stimulate her into a second orgasm when she was still coming down from the first. She shuddered beneath him, her muscles tightening around him, and he felt the nano-bots re-enter his body. He didn't need to collect any data on her — she wasn't slated to be a Bride — but he'd look at the information later, anyway, just in case. He knew that if anybody did an audit on this mission, he'd catch a reprimand at best for having probed the client's little sister, but he could take some heat. Everything had been worth it.

He pulled out of her and then rolled to his side, closing his eyes. Without opening them, he put his arms around her and kissed her. He thought that he caught her ear.

"Good way to wake up."

He could feel her turning in his arms, and then her soft mouth was touching his, her tongue asking for entrance. He opened his mouth to accept her, and she intertwined her tongue with his. They kissed like that for several minutes before she pulled back.

"Wow, I never thought intimacy would be like that."

"Were you untouched?"

"Yes. Was I okay?"

"Okay?" How could he explain to her that he'd never felt the heights of pleasure that he'd just experienced. "You were more than okay. You blew my mind."

She kissed him again, hard and fast. Then she pulled herself out of his arms, despite a quick grab to keep her in the circle of his arms.

"Thank you, but I need to clean up. I'm sticky."

Xun opened his eyes and looked at his naked lover walk towards the sonic shower.

"I guess I should come, too."

Alarms

Illary

Xun followed her into the sonic
shower. Illary turned it on. The two of
them stood inside, waiting as the
sonic waves cleaned their bodies.
Xun leaned down and kissed Illary,
then he pulled her up and pinned her
against the wall as he ravaged her
mouth again and again. Illary liked
the way that he tasted, and she
opened her mouth and tilted her

head as the kiss grew more
passionate.

They were interrupted by the
blaring of loud alarms. Illary put her
hands over her ears.

Xun immediately put Illary back
onto her feet.

"Stay here. I'm going to check on
what's happening."

Xun pulled on his uniform in half
a second and was out the door before
Illary could even react.

She supposed that she should
get dressed, too. She couldn't

remember all that much of last night, only that she'd tried to proposition Xun...and she'd followed through this morning, waking up, getting naked, and initiating sex.

What a first time! She went to find the clothing that she'd discarded and put it back on. Her clothes weren't all that clean, but at least her skin was.

The door opened as Xun came in. He turned around and double locked it.

"What's going on?"

Xun's mouth was grim. "Space pirates."

Illary blinked. "What? What are space pirates?"

"They pillage space stations like this one. It's not particularly secure, especially not during the convention. They thought that they were too small to be noticed, but obviously that was not true."

"What are we going to do?" Illary noticed how she thought of them as a unit.

"We have to clear the station

before our ship arrives. Space pirates going onto Intara would be disastrous. Of course their soldiers can repel nearly any attack, but I'd rather not take even the 1% chance that they'd come back to Intara and wreak havoc there."

"How are you going to do that?"

"I'm going to rally some troops. Stay in the room, okay? If I knock once, then you'll know that it's not me. Three knocks and you open the door."

Illary nodded. She knew that she

should be more scared — she'd never heard of space pirates, let alone fought them — but Xun seemed like it was normal. Maybe it was normal for him, but Illary had been imprisoned in a temple for most of her life, so she wasn't used to quite this much excitement.

He leaned in and kissed her hard before sprinting to the door, unlocking it, and going into the hallway. Illary locked the door after him.

She was exhausted from their

vigorous morning sex, and she lay

down on the bed. There wasn't much

for her to do but worry, so she might

as well rest while she could.

Bravery

Xun

Xun quickly descended to a lower level of the station. He understood how he would coordinate an attack on a space station like this, even with a limited number of men. Deep in the heart of the station, where they'd gone to the fight, there was a lot of space that the pirates wouldn't bother supervising; it wasn't tactically important, far from any power supply or the control room. Anybody with Xun's training or anything like it would convene there.

When he was there, he was relieved to find dozens of men with military posture. He hadn't admitted to himself that he nearly went on a suicide mission in order to get Illary off of this station.

"You're with KSM?" One of the Jalan warriors was looking at the logo on Xun's suit.

"Yeah."

"Got any bright ideas?"

"Sure. I'd like to hear your plans first."

He was met with a sea of blank faces.

"We're soldiers, not strategists."

"Surely you've been trained in this sort of thing. You're here, after all."

"Aren't you supposed to be the best? Tell us your plan, and we'll tell you if we'll follow you."

Xun nodded. He needed to handle these men for Illary's safety. He was grateful that Phuoc and

Suyana weren't here, even though Illary had been upset about it.

"Here's what I'm planning. We need to scout to see where their center of activity is. They'll set up an HQ somewhere. Could be the control room, could be elsewhere."

"And then what?"

"And then we kill them."

There was a roar from the warriors, a war cry that Xun felt in his bones. He smiled for the first time since the alarms had sounded. He'd be able to figure things out. Illary would be safe.

* * *

Two hours later, Xun was belly-crawling in an air duct. He looked out through a vent to see dozens upon dozens of space pirates eating food from the dining area. They were having some kind of meeting, a hologram of the nearest planet rotating in front of them with certain spots marked. The space station was too insignificant to protect, but the pirates were apparently intent on attacking a nearby planet while using the station as a home base.

"You have the grenade?" The Jalan warrior he'd spoken to first had become an unspoken second-in-command.

"Yeah." He handed the smoke grenade to Xun.

"Close your eyes. Don't get any of it in your eyes." He pulled out the pin and threw it down into the dining area. The men covered their eyes as best they could. Tear gas was nasty stuff, but it was necessary when they were out-manned.

Xun waited for a minute for the tear gas to dissipate, then he attached a rope to one part of the air duct before rappelling down. A good leader always went first into any kind of action.

He was met with a space pirate's knife, a large one that looked like a hunting knife. It cut his calf. Carefully balancing on mostly one leg, he fought hand to hand with the pirate, who could barely see. Xun pulled out his laser gun, but he couldn't get the time to calibrate it properly with the pirate blindly swinging a knife, which was more effective than Xun would've expected.

"Behind you!"

Xun spun around and smacked the oncoming pirate in the face with the butt of his gun, knocking the pirate out cold. He turned and calibrated his gun so that he could incapacitate the first pirate.

But the first pirate had taken advantage of the distraction to get even closer to Xun, and now he was able to slash Xun's midsection, cutting Xun's guts. Both of them knew that this kind of wound was fatal.

Xun was wearing a KSM uniform, which was mostly useless against knives. They could handle high-speed projectiles and lasers, but knives were beyond their ability.

Xun fell to his knees. He saw his second slay the pirate who had cut him, but it was already too late for Xun. He sank back, one hand on his bleeding mid-section.

He'd failed Illary.

Opposite

Illary

Illary knew that Xun had told her to stay in her room, but she couldn't bear to sit there and do nothing. Her nap hadn't lasted as long as she would have liked, and Xun could probably use her help. She wasn't any good in battle, but she was very good for the aftermath. Spread across a lot of men, she could only use a little bit of power, but she'd be able to address the biggest things until the medical healers at this convention could help whoever had confronted the space pirates.

Illary could hear shouting coming from the dining area. Her heart pounded hard as she came closer. She was at the upper balcony now, and she cautiously looked down, staying hidden by crouching low.

The fighting was fierce. The space pirates' eyes were barely open and streaming tears, but they were fighting the station's defenders nonetheless.

Her heart stopped when she saw that Xun's intestines had been cut. He was bleeding and spilling fluids on the ground. She didn't care about the fighting. She had to get down to him.

Running for the stairs, she flew down them, quickly running out to tend to Xun before he died.

"No," she gasped, out of breath as she ran faster than she ever had. She couldn't think about her lover dying so soon after they finally came together.

Then she was down at the level of the fighting. She ignored it, not moving an inch as a space pirate came at her with a machete that was raised. A Jalan warrior growled and engaged the pirate personally. Illary had more important things to do than worry about fighting.

She knelt beside Xun's body. His eyes were closed, but his chest was still rising and falling. He was still alive.

"Xun," she said. "Talk to me."

His eyes opened a crack. "Illary?"

"Xun."

"Get out of here. Not safe."

"I don't care." Illary put her hand on his midsection. He pushed her hand away.

"Stop it! I'm trying to help you."

"You'll die beside me. I can't bear that. Go now."

"Stop." Illary closed her eyes and concentrated. She hadn't healed anybody since she left the temple, but she knew how to after years of doing it multiple times a day every day. Kaley could heal many people with just a song, but Illary had to touch the patient. She thought about his body knitting back together, everything going back into the proper place.

"I'm not bleeding anymore." Xun's voice was louder now. "What did you do?"

"I'm a healer."

"Not for long."

Illary turned as she heard a voice behind her. A huge space pirate with a scar where his right ear should be was raising a gigantic machete. Xun was still behind her.

She could feel a rush of energy going through her, and she was filled with new ferocity. He shouldn't be attacking a healer and a patient.

She got to her feet, holding out her hand as if she were going to heal him.

He laughed and swung the machete, only for it to drop from his hand. He looked at his hand, which was beginning to blister.

"What..."

He fell on the ground, his body

writhing and convulsing as Illary cooked him from the inside out. She imagined all of his organs failing, his blood boiling, and his heart stopping. She held her breath. She didn't know if it would work.

Then his head went to the side, and she knew he was dead. He wasn't breathing anymore. She knelt next to him and checked his pulse by putting two fingers on his neck. Dead for sure.

Illary still had all that energy inside of her, and she spread her arms wide as she screamed her rage at the pirates who had dared to hurt her lover. She was angry enough to make all of their blood boil as much as hers did, filled with the fire of her rage.

For a moment, nothing happened. Then, one by one, the pirates fell as their bodies betrayed them and their blood boiled in their veins, hastening their deaths.

A roar rose from the station's defenders, who took advantage of the moment to slay each and every pirate in the room.

Overcome by the largest thing

that she'd ever done, Illary fainted.

Transport

Illary

Illary woke up several hours later in a room that she'd never seen before.

"Where am I?"

"We're in the transport. Whatever you did knocked you out for several hours. I don't think that you should do it again."

She pressed her lips together. "I'd do it again in a heartbeat."

He waited for a moment before saying, "Thank you for saving my life."

"You're welcome."

She sat up and looked around the room. "So you brought me to the transport ship to Intara? Where is all of our stuff?"

"I had someone look out for you while I grabbed things from our room and brought them to the space dock. Not all of the pirates were in that room, and it took some time to round them all up. I've left it in the hands of people who belonged on that station; I have to say that their security practices are pretty loose. Anyway, let's just stay in bed until we get to Intara, hmm?" He looked at her with a certain light in his eyes, and she smiled back up at him.

"I think I get what you're saying." She licked her lips and moved towards him. She straddled his body and put her thighs on the outside of his hips. His big hands gripped her cheeks and brought her even closer to him. She could feel the ridge of his erection through his uniform.

She leaned down to kiss him and her hair fell in a curtain around the two of them. She brushed it back before kissing him lightly and then even more aggressively, using her tongue to tease and tantalize him. She kissed all the way to his ear and bit it before trailing down to his neck and biting him fiercely there, too.

She found herself rolled onto her back, her thighs still around his body. He was taking off his uniform now, and the pants of her uniform were pulled down so that she was naked from the waist down. He moved down her body, kissing the soft skin of her lower stomach before licking her wet core.

"Oh!" Her hips surged upward; she could feel herself getting wetter.

His hands were holding her thighs hard enough to bruise, but she didn't mind. She loved the intensity of their love-making. His tongue caressed her gently, painting fire between her thighs, and one hand left her thigh to enter her lower lips.

Then she found herself flipped over, facedown on the bed, and she felt him pull her legs so that she was bent at the knee. He pushed inside of her, and she moaned into the pillow.

"So good."

He pushed her legs apart even wider as he picked up the pace, and her moans increased in volume. Then he was pulling her hair so that her back was arched, her whole body quaking with the force of a strong orgasm.

Xun shouted behind her as he released inside of her body. He put a hand under her to stimulate her clitoris, rubbing it in tight circles. She found her muscles clenching yet again as she found completion for a second time in the space of a few minutes.

Xun pulled out of her then and kissed her shoulder.

"Do you want to clean up?"

"No. I just want to stay here and bask in the glorious sensation of being loved like this."

She could hear Xun swallow hard.

"I love you."

"I love you, too."

Xun was very quiet after they exchanged the words, but she knew that he meant it. She felt him pick her up to bring her into the sonic shower. He bent down to kiss her again, and there was a little desperation in his kiss, as if they wouldn't have much time. But they had all the time in the universe. Surely he'd stay with her on Intara.

She didn't want to ruin their blossoming relationship with too many questions, though, so she kept quiet.

When they got out of the sonic shower, as he got dressed again, he told her, "I need to run a few errands, okay? There are a few things that I need to check on this ship. You'll be fine here. I want you to rest, though. That blast of whatever you did really took a lot out of you."

"I'll wait here this time," she promised.

"I'll see you later." He kissed her nose and then he was gone.

Heat

Illary

Since she was alone, she could test out her new-found powers. She'd always had unreliable telekinesis, but the power to heat was something totally new. She concentrated on building a small ball of warmth between her hands, and she felt her eyebrows shoot upwards when the lights in the room flickered. She let the power course through her veins;

she knew that Xun didn't want her to push it, but it felt pretty wonderful.

Her mother had always been a healer, and their father wasn't a fighter. She'd never even thought about using her powers to fight, and she knew that her mother would be appalled that she'd used the gift of healing to kill people.

Illary had been a healer for so long that she didn't or couldn't think of herself as anyone else. In a way, her forced job had been her identity, and she didn't know who she was at her core without it. She never meant to become a murderer.

Illary stared at her hands, which were physically blood free; she knew that she had blood on them, though, blood which she could never wash off. She had no idea that she could kill people, but she was glad that she'd been able to save Xun and herself during the space pirate attack.

The ball of warmth between her hands was now expanding like a miniature sun through little rays everywhere. Beams of light spread to illuminate the room and the adjacent bathroom. The room was heating up, as if she was heating those objects in addition to the light. Gasping, she let the light die. What could she do?

Kaley had always been the strongest of them, but now Illary wondered if Kaley's expanded abilities were due to her age. As far as she knew, Illary hadn't been able to do this kind of thing when they were kids. She was unlocking new powers as she aged.

She closed her eyes and rested,

but she couldn't fall asleep. Her mind was racing with the possibilities of the new powers that she'd been able to use.

The door opened as Xun came back. She looked at him, tucking away the shred of guilt; she really hadn't followed his orders.

"How do you feel about dance exhibitions?"

"I've never been to one. I used to dance a lot with my sisters, though."

Xun smiled and came to kiss her cheek gently. "Then let's go to the dance exhibition that they have going

on tonight."

Dance Exhibition

Xun

Xun kept a hand on Illary's waist as they walked to the dance hall. There wasn't much room there, but Xun pushed his way through to find two seats that were together near the very top. He kept an arm around her; he'd make the most of their time together.

The lights were off, which made the glowing stones on the walls shine a little brighter. They were Intaran light crystals. Xun had to admit that the effect was pretty stunning.

Then a single spotlight came to the center of the stage, where two people were standing. One was tall and male, while the second was small and female. They began to dance in sync, doing the same moves. Then they began to interact, the male picking the female up and tossing her in the air before catching her in his arms. She slid down his body in a way that made Xun's pants feel a little tighter.

Still keeping one arm around Illary, he used his other hand to adjust himself. He hoped that Illary was too caught up in the exhibition to notice.

But her hand found its way to his knee, which didn't help the situation. He could smell her when she was this close, and her scent had some kind of effect on him.

He stopped breathing when he thought about the implications of her scent being this intoxicating. No. He couldn't be mated to the sister of the client. It wasn't allowed. Just being involved wasn't allowed; having a long-term relationship or mating her forever definitely wasn't allowed. If he wanted to make his way up the KSM ranks to the position of prober, one of the highest ranks, then he needed to stay unattached.

Illary was very tempting, though. He watched as the couple on the stage passed each other, flirting but not touching, walking close to their partner and spinning after their tumultuous part together. Slowly, they came closer and closer on each pass, until they were nearly touching. Then the girl lifted her leg to the guy's shoulder and brought him close to her body, their faces only a hairsbreadth apart. He lifted her by her waist, and she swung her legs together before arching her back and making a perfect curve with her body. The male dancer set her on her feet. The two bowed to the audience.

Xun was more than uncomfortable at this point. He was

far too aroused for a public space, and he hoped that nobody noticed.

"Let's get out of here," he whispered into Illary's ear.

"Okay."

He took her hand in his and brought her out of the room.

Holo Sea

Illary

Xun pulled Illary into the nearest room, dark with no one inside. Xun flicked on the lights.

"It's a Holo Sea."

"What's that?"

"It shows your thoughts."

"How?"

"You stand in the marked spot and imagine a landscape, and it'll come to life all around you."

"I want to try!" Illary moved towards the big blue dot on the floor. Instantly, she closed her eyes and thought about one of the mythical large oceans that were the stuff of legends. There were old, old tales about mer-folk.

"Open your eyes."

She could see her imagined ocean around them. Kaley was always better at illusions, and Illary had never been able to make scenes before. The Holo Sea was almost as good as actually being able to create illusions.

She thought about turning herself into a half-fish, half-woman. And then she did and she had a fake tail around her. She giggled as she turned Xun, a serious soldier, into a half-fish, half-man. He pretended to swim over to her, and she was glad that he was indulging her bit of childish whimsy. She'd missed out on a lot of the games that she might have played as a young child.

He embraced her, kissing her and pulling her close.

"You're a beautiful mermaid," he murmured before kissing her again. She couldn't keep the image of the mer-people in her mind anymore, but she didn't mind. Her clothes were falling to the floor now, and Xun was already naked. He held her as he pulled her down in a controlled fall, taking the brunt of it on his back. She was astride him, and he guided himself inside of her. She'd gotten aroused by watching the flirtation on the stage and seeing Xun's reaction to it. She was glad that he'd pulled her out of the big room and into the Holo Sea.

She rolled her hips, her eyes closing as the intensity of the sensation swept throughout her body.

"Faster."

Xun's hands were on her hips now, urging her to pick up the pace. She rocked back and forth on him now, panting hard, and then white light filled her head as she finished. Xun grunted as he released inside of her, and he put a hand on her clit to push her once more into a second orgasm.

When she opened her eyes, she could see a crumbling temple behind him. Xun was dressed in a different uniform than the one that he'd worn today.

"What's that?"

Xun twisted to look at what the Holo Sea was projecting.

"No idea why there's a temple there."

Illary wasn't a seer — that was Kaley — but she might have just seen a vision of the future.

"We should get out of here before someone sees us." She didn't want to tell him that she was spooked by the first flash of her precognition. It was enough that she could apparently transfer heat; she didn't need to learn that she could also see the future.

Shopping

Illary

The next morning, Illary's arms were bursting with items, nearly too many for her to carry. Her heart was full of joy. Xun had given her a credit pass and told her to use as much as she liked. It would be paid for by Kaley.

She still didn't know how much Kaley had, but she thought that the limit must be high if she could buy

what she liked. If Kaley wasn't rich —
and how could she be poor if she
really was a queen — Illary would pay
off whatever debt she amassed.

The stores were full of trinkets
and items that she'd never seen
before. She felt like a small child in a
sweet shop. She tasted samples and
tried new gadgets with abandon,
making her way through each store
before moving onto the next.

When she couldn't shop
anymore, she rested in a small café,
drinking xocolatl and enjoying a little

people-watching. She could hear the conversation of the people next to her.

"The sensitives boarding today are the closest things to angels in the universe. I've made every possible preparation for their arrival."

Awed, she cocked her head. She'd never met an angel. There were many things in the universe that she'd never known even existed.

She turned to look back at the main corridor. Before her was a tall man with hair that appeared like a burning flame. A golden sword was sheathed at his side, and he had big, white wings. She sputtered. He looked exactly like the religious images that the Alhmanics kept in their temple.

"Hello," she managed.

He nodded at her before moving past her and speaking to the people at the next table in a language she didn't speak. It definitely wasn't Standard. It sounded like the chiming of bells, almost as if he were singing. She didn't know why she knew that he was a male, but she knew it in her bones.

She checked the time on the watch that Xun insisted that she buy. She needed to meet him somewhere. He'd told her before he left this morning that there was something that he wanted to show her, since she'd liked the Holo Sea so much.

She hurried back to their room, dumping all of her purchases in a big heap on the floor. She quickly swiped through the guide to find their meeting point, and then she walked quickly there.

Xun was already there when she arrived.

"Did you have a good time shopping?"

"The best. I only wish that Suyana and Kaley were there to share it." She frowned. She'd barely thought of her sisters. She'd been frantic when Suyana had first disappeared, but now it seemed like part of another life. She was stealing a little time away from her real responsibilities while she journeyed with Xun, and a small part of her wished that it would never end.

Nonsense, of course. She knew that she'd end up on Intara with Kaley and probably Suyana, if Xun was right about Phuoc's abilities to handle Suyana. Suyana had leaned on Illary for their whole lives. What must she be going through when she was totally abandoned by both sisters?

"I want to show you another body of water today."

Illary shook away the thoughts of

her sisters. She had no power to change anything while she was on the ship, so she might as well enjoy herself and push the guilt away.

"What is it?"

"It's formed of coded nanites. It's supposed to have the effect of wine on the mind when the water wets your skin."

"I can't wait."

Xun pulled her into the room. "I reserved it just for us for the next few hours."

Illary looked around. "I don't

have a bathing suit." On Kador, as a child, she hadn't needed one. When she'd gotten a little older, she grew shy enough to preserve some of her modesty before she'd been imprisoned in the temple.

"You don't need one. I've seen your naked body before. Nobody will disturb us."

Illary felt Xun pull her clothes off until she was naked.

"Get in the pool."

She hurried to obey, carefully going down the small steps into the wet pool.

It really did feel like water and swimming, but she felt that pure happiness caused by the Intaran wine fill her. Xun was naked now, and he joined her inside of the pool.

She had a thought that she wished that her sisters were here to enjoy the beautiful pool with glimmering rocks set around it. She hoped that Suyana was enjoying wherever she was just as much as Illary was enjoying this ship. She kept a little bit of worry in her mind, but it was hard to pay attention when the dizzying effects of the pool made her so happy.

She gasped as something moved next to her.

"What was that?"

"It's a bio-engineered fish. They glow."

Illary whipped around, trying to see another one. She could see the little fish moving beneath the surface of the water, and Xun picked her up in his arms and spun her around as the little fish darted around them. He brought her close for a deep kiss, and then she was sliding down his body.

She could tell from the way that he was breathing that he was aroused, so she put her hand around the base of his cock. He was fully erect; she tugged him until his eyes were closed.

"Have to be inside of you."

She turned around so that her back was facing him. She put her hands on the edge of the pool and bent over. He pushed inside of her without much foreplay; he was probably too far gone to tease her. But the calming and relaxing effects of the pool helped her accept him inside of her body very easily.

The nanite water moved around them more slowly than real water as Xun plunged in and out of her ready body. She felt as if the ball of heat that she'd made before was inside of her core. Finally, Xun spilled inside of her, triggering her own orgasm shortly after.

"Let's go back to our room," Xun whispered in Illary's ear. "Then we can do more."

They got out of the water and got

dressed before going back to their

room, hand in hand.

Vomit

Illary

When Illary woke up the next morning, she was sick to her stomach. Xun was nowhere to be found. She hurried to the bathroom and emptied her stomach inside of the toilet. She felt like death.

What was going on? Where was Xun?

She rinsed her mouth out with a little mouthwash before going back into the room. She could see that the screen of their room's terminal was glowing. She tapped it.

Meeting with KSM. Back after lunch. Order whatever you want.

It seemed that she'd been left on her own. She'd enjoyed her shopping spree the day before — wonderful after what seemed like an eternity of burlap dresses for the purity of her soul — but she wasn't in the mood to wander around the ship, especially if she was going to spontaneously barf.

She bit her lip. She didn't know if

the ship had healers who were better than her. She went to the bathroom and rummaged around in the drawers until she found a small diagnosis wand.

She waved it over her stomach. The hologram instantly said that she was pregnant. She could see an image of the little baby nestled inside of her.

Xun could lose his job over this. She'd seduced him, yes, but he had superiors to answer to. If they wanted to, he could lose everything for fraternizing with her. She was afraid that he might be angry about the baby. What if he wanted nothing to do with the two of them?

She ordered simple flatbread from the room service, which would send a bot over with her freshly prepared food. There was a replicator in her room for simple things, but she wanted something a little better from the specialized bots in the dining hall. Soon, she had the flatbread that she wanted. She ate it in small bites as she thought through the implications of being pregnant with Xun's child.

She knew that the Kadorians rarely had morning sickness quite this early in a pregnancy. Whatever was going on with her body was some kind of reaction with Xun's heritage. She had no idea what the gestation period was for his species; if she was already having morning sickness this early, would that mean that the baby would continue to develop at an accelerated pace?

She put her hand on her stomach as she waited for Xun to

come back.

Loss

Xun

When Xun came back into the
room, he steeled himself to tell Illary
that KSM required her to be
examined by a healer. She'd been
tired out by killing the pirates, and
the healers employed by KSM insisted
that Illary have a clean bill of health
before they delivered her. It wouldn't
be good for their reputation if they
delivered her in worse shape than

they'd found her.

Xun opened the door to their room to see Illary sitting on the bed. She was short enough that her feet didn't touch the ground.

"Hello."

Illary got to her feet and threw herself into his arms, her head resting against his chest.

"Are you okay?"

"I have to talk to you."

"Okay." He tugged her towards the bed with his hands on her waist. "Tell me."

"Promise you won't be mad."

"Promise."

"I'm pregnant."

Xun sat there, totally stunned for just a moment. Then he leaned forward and kissed Illary, the mother of his child.

"That's fantastic news!" It was shocking that Illary had been fertile, and it was doubly shocking that she'd gotten pregnant from him. All KSM employees regularly took a drug that rendered them sterile. It happened every week.

He thought back to the last time that he'd taken it...and he realized that he hadn't taken the pills with him when they evacuated the big KSM ship after the attack. His body had enough time to get it out of his system, and now Illary was pregnant with his kid.

He held her close and stroked her back. "So happy." But as he smelled the sweet scent of her hair, he felt worry in his gut. Losing his job would be the least of his worry, on Intara, he could be arrested for touching the queen's sister.

"Illary, I have something to tell you, too."

"What?"

"KSM has requested that you submit to an examination by a local healer before you are delivered to your sister."

Illary was still in his arms.

"They'll hear about the baby."

"Yes."

"What will happen?"

"I don't know. It could be okay."

"It won't be, though."

"Probably not."

Illary scooted back until she could see his face.

"What should we do?"

"We're keeping the baby," Xun told her firmly. "I'd rather lose my job than lose our baby. But I'm not sure what kind of punishment I'll get for this."

"There's not much that we can do, is there?"

"Not a lot of options, Illary."

Xun was understating what would happen. He knew that he

would probably face some jail time on Intara for taking Illary's virginity, but he couldn't have resisted her charms. He would only hope that jail wouldn't make Illary leave him for someone else.

Medical Bay

Illary

The next morning, Illary jiggled her leg as she waited in the medical bay.

"I'll be right with you," the healer called. "Just a few minutes."

Illary could hear a baby's cry, and her heart tightened at the sound. The baby sounded purely miserable; she hoped that the baby was okay. She sounded pretty sick, which Illary guessed was the reason why the baby was in the healer's area.

She was amazed to have the little life growing inside of her. She was glad that Xun was the father, but she didn't know if he'd be by her side while she raised her child. How would they clear him with his superiors? Once the test results were sent to KSM, they would know that Illary and Xun were lovers.

Kaley was a queen, so she could get Xun out of any punishment, right? Illary hoped that Kaley wouldn't judge Xun too harshly for loving Illary. She could feel in her gut that something was going to go wrong. Her precognition wasn't very trained, so she couldn't see what would happen exactly, but she still had a bad feeling about the not so distant future.

Then the crying baby was moving away and the healer entered Illary's room.

"Okay, dear?"

"Yes, ma'am." Illary tried not to look as nervous as she felt.

"It's okay," the healer said, noticing Illary's hands twisting together. "Nothing will be too invasive. I'm just going to use a wand, if that's okay."

Illary nodded quickly. Here was the moment of truth.

She was still as the healer did a thorough check of Illary's entire body. Information popped up on her screen.

"Congratulations! You're pregnant!" The nurse winked at her. "You'll be a good mother, I can tell."

Illary had no clue how the nurse

could possibly know that, but she nodded mutely anyway. She could feel sweat breaking out on her forehead from the stress of having her pregnancy confirmed by a healer.

"Advanced pregnancy. You're about a third of the way through the gestation cycle. When did you get pregnant?"

"A few days ago," Illary whispered.

The healer frowned. "This baby is pretty advanced for conception a few days ago. Are you sure?"

Illary nodded. "I lost my virginity a few days ago."

The healer was quiet. "It must be a species I haven't treated yet, then." She flipped through the information on her screen.

"Nothing else is popping up. You're good to go. I'll forward this report to KSM."

"Thank you," she told the healer, though she didn't feel thankful at all. The healer was just doing her job. "I appreciate it."

"You're welcome! If you have any

questions about pregnancy, I'm here to help. I have two of my own."

Illary shook the healer's offered hand before walking back to her room in a daze. KSM would know now.

Slow Love

Illary

Illary walked back to the room in a daze. Everything was out of her hands now. She opened the door, and Xun came to kiss her as soon as he noticed that she'd come inside.

"You okay? Everything's fine?"

She nodded.

"The healer confirmed my pregnancy." Her lower lip trembled. She didn't want to cry.

"Hey." Xun swept her into his arms and held her close before picking her up entirely and bringing her to the bed. "We'll find a way through this."

She wrapped her arms around his solid body and smelled his masculine scent. It comforted her a little bit, but she knew that their troubles weren't over by a long shot. She realized that her hands were shaking a little bit.

"I just wish that we were having a baby in other circumstances."

He kissed her temple. "Me, too."

"But I don't regret our child."

"Of course not."

Illary's tears spilled down her cheeks now. A tear drop fell on Xun's hand, so he leaned back so that he could see her crying.

"Nothing to cry about. We'll get through this together."

"But I just don't know what's going to happen. Suyana has never been apart from me this long, and Kaley's probably worried if she heard about the space pirate attack. And now I have a baby and you might lose your job and…"

Xun cut her litany of worries off with a deep kiss, crushing their lips together. Then she felt him removing her clothes and then his own. She watched him come back to bed and wrap his whole body around hers.

"Everything will be fine. I promise."

She knew that he couldn't promise something like that, but she took the comfort for what it was worth. She kissed him softly and wrapped her leg around his lower body.

His hips surged into the cradle of her thighs. She moved her leg a little higher on his hips as he pushed inside of her body.

They held each other as they made slow, sweet love right there in the bed. They might only have a short time together, and both of them knew that they had to make the most of it. When Illary got to Intara, she'd get her sisters back, but the price was probably Xun's job and possibly freedom.

Xun interrupted Illary's thoughts by saying, "We shouldn't stay in bed the entire day."

Illary groaned wordlessly.

He spanked her lightly.

"Come into the shower with me. We're going to have some fun outside of this room."

"Should we really be seen together? Isn't that making it worse? Maybe we should just stay in the room."

Instead of answering, he pulled

her into his arms and took her to the sonic shower to clean up. This time, it was business-like, the two of them waiting for the sonic waves to clean their bodies. Then they went back to their bedroom and got dressed.

"There's a dance game that I'm sure you'll love."

"Where is it?"

"It's on the lower deck. There's a tournament today."

"I'm not that good at dancing," she warned Xun. "I can watch while you participate."

"No chance. Everybody has to be partnered up for the competition."

"Why?"

"You'll see."

Dance Competition

Illary

They left their room and went to a lower deck, which was slightly crowded. There was a bunch of people around some kind of registration table, and Xun brought out a credit pass to pay for their entry.

"What's the prize?"

"These floating flowers."

Illary looked at them in wonder.

"Wow, those are so pretty."

The registration man snorted. "You don't get out much, do you?"

Xun scowled at him.

"Come on," he told Illary, his arm around her shoulders. "Let's get into position."

Another person wearing the same color shirt as the man who had handled their registration came forward with a ribbon.

"I'll just tie you together now."

"What?" Xun blinked. "Like a wedding?"

"No, not like a wedding. I'm tying your ankles together. It's a three-legged dance."

The man quickly knelt and tied Illary and Xun's ankles together so that they were a three-legged monster. They hobbled the rest of the way to their station.

"Attention, contestants," a big voice boomed. "Blossoms of light will appear on your dance board. Whoever succeeds in stomping the most light will win the prize. Good luck."

Xun and Illary watched as light began to appear at their station while music played. They looked over at their neighbors and saw how they were using their partners' bodies to balance, so they did the same. It was weird and awkward at first — Illary wondered if they'd break the ribbon — but once they got into a good rhythm, it was fun. Illary had never played any kind of dance game like this, so she cut loose and enjoyed herself. She concentrated on hitting each light. It seemed that each light was as far away and as difficult to access as possible; when they were tied together, they were much slower than when they were moving singly. But Illary knew Xun's body almost as well as her own at this point, which definitely helped.

Then the music stopped.

"And the winners are...Contestants 525!"

Illary looked around at the numbers of their neighbors, but she didn't see the number 525. Xun was pulling her forward.

"What? I was trying to see who won."

"We did."

Xun pulled the registration packet out of his pocket. "We're 525."

"We won!" Illary wanted to jump into Xun's arms, but their legs were still tied together, so she settled for a quick squeeze of his midsection.

They were able to quickly make their way to the registration table, where they were presented with flowers while everyone clapped. Then Xun bent to untie their ankles. They walked hand in hand back to their room with Illary carrying the floating flowers, which smelled like a heavenly garden.

When they got back inside of their room, Xun turned to Illary.

"I want you to know something."

"Yes?"

"Tonight is our last night before we reach Intara, but I want you to know that I am in love with you. You and the baby are worth any sacrifice that I need to make, okay?"

Illary's eyes filled with tears.

"I understand."

Xun kissed her gently and held her close.

"Just remember that when we get to Intara."

Detained

Illary

As soon as they arrived on Intara, Xun brought Illary out of the ship so that she could see her sisters. The second that he stepped on Intaran soil, two Intaran guards came to clap handcuffs on him.

"Get those off of him!" Illary snapped. "The nerve!"

"We can't, lady." One guard was leading Xun away from her, and Xun wasn't struggling. "KSM orders. They want us to detain Xun pending an internal investigation."

Illary felt as if her heart had been stabbed. Would KSM tear them apart? Her eyes filled with tears.

"You have to release him," she said, her voice thick.

"Listen, that's beyond our abilities. I can give you an official request form for release, but those are processed very slowly. There's not much that you can do. Are you mated or married to this man?"

"No," she whispered.

"Then there's no point in filing this form at all."

"I'm coming with you," she announced.

The guard shrugged. "We won't stop you. There are benches for people who are waiting."

Illary walked with them, battling both anger and grief. Anger because they were detaining her lover and grief because she was fully aware that they might lock Xun away and take him off-planet, where she could not follow him.

* * *

Four hours later, she had a conversation for the fifth time.

"Lady, you'd really be more comfortable in the room we have for this kind of thing. There's a couch. You can eat some snacks while he's processed."

"I'm fine," Illary said. Her stomach was growling since she hadn't eaten for a long time, but somehow she just didn't care enough to eat, which said a lot since she'd been steadily deprived of food while she was in the temple.

She wouldn't feel hungry until Xun was free, and it was looking like the possibility was slipping away with each hour. She hadn't seen him since they'd gotten to this office; she was afraid that she might not see him ever again, which was why she refused to move. What if moving her into a room was a ploy to keep her trapped and separated from him as they moved him somewhere else?

Not even for Suyana and Kaley's

sake would she move from this bench. Where was Kaley, anyway? Illary felt a surge of anger which made her cheeks heat. The lights in the office flickered, but she didn't care. Wasn't Kaley supposed to help navigate this kind of thing?

Xun hadn't done anything wrong. How could falling in love be wrong? She didn't understand how things were done on Intara, but it seemed to her that if two people were in love...nothing should come between them.

Sneaking Out

Illary

Five hours later, the guards had forced Illary to go into a nearby building and stay in her room. Her door was locked, but her window certainly wasn't. They really had not planned ahead when they put her on the ground floor.

When night fell, Illary was out the window. She was still for a moment, waiting to see if they had any kind of surveillance out there.

They didn't seem to have anything. She went back to the office where she'd sat on that bench for several hours. She knew where they were keeping Xun, though they hadn't let her go back. She looked through the windows of each holding cell, which all had bars over them, until she finally found the one with Xun inside of it.

"Xun!"

"Illary?"

Xun got to his feet and came to

his window.

"Illary, don't endanger yourself and our child by being out here. Go back to wherever you're being kept."

"No!" She put her hand flat on the window, and Xun reciprocated on the other side of the glass. "My sister will come. She can fix things."

"The news from KSM came. They sent somebody, but there was a solar storm that forced them to dock not too long after they left. I'm going to be in here for a while."

"Kaley can get you out," she said,

with much more confidence than she felt. "She can get everything cleared up."

Lights went on outside of the office.

"Who's out there?"

Illary's heart beat quickly. She'd been caught.

She ran back towards the building where she'd been, but she was quickly tackled by an Intaran guard, one of the men who had seen her earlier.

"It's you," he said, not sounding

particularly surprised or alarmed.

"How did you get out?"

"My secret."

"I'll escort you back."

Illary turned back to see Xun watching the scene from inside of his cell. The guard had a hand on Illary's upper arm; he dragged her back to the nearby building. This time, he saw that the window was open.

"We should've locked the window. Let me fix that."

He took some kind of key out of his pocket and sealed the window.

Now Illary really was trapped in her room.

"Lady, you'll stay in here until your sister comes. Good thing that she's a queen, or you'd be facing a lot worse for trying to talk to a prisoner."

"He's not a prisoner! He's just temporarily detained!"

"Good night, lady."

The door was shut. Illary could hear the thumps that the locks made as they slid home.

Illary hugged herself. What could she do to help Xun?

Liaison

Xun

Xun's cell door opened, and a man came inside.

"You're Xun?"

"Yes, sir." Xun knew that the KSM officer coming inside of his cell had to be of a very high rank, maybe even prober status. He had special stars on his uniform to indicate that he was part of the internal audit team.

"I'm Xerxes, the investigator in charge of your case."

"Investigator?"

"We're concerned about Illary's pregnancy. Fraternization between a KSM employee and his charge is against the rules...a very serious offense."

Xun felt his hackles rise. "Surely there's a loophole in the rules for falling in love."

"Love is easily confused with lust."

Xun shook his head. "I know

what love is, and I know that I have it with Illary."

Xerxes seemed to soften just a hair.

"I'll tell you what I'll do. We can open this up to a wider part of the KSM community. If you would agree to a trial with a jury of your peers, then we can make this public, or as public as the internal workings of KSM can get."

"I agree."

"I'll put together the paperwork and send it your way. There is one more thing."

"What?"

"KSM's proprietary nano-bots are still in your system."

"Yes, they are. What about it?"

"We're going to need those back."

Xun blinked. "How exactly are you going to extract them?"

Xerxes brought a small container out of his carrying case.

"We'll need you to deposit the nano-bots into this."

"But we can't deposit our seed into anything but a living female…we can't get them back without a female orgasm."

"Yes."

Xun understood now what the investigator was asking him to do.

The investigator cleared his throat. "If you're reinstated, you'll be re-injected with the bots. Until then, you need to give them up. We can't have them floating around on Intara, you see."

"Can I have some privacy?"

"I'll be back in two minutes."

He walked to the door and got

out. Xun heard the door lock again. He stared out the window where Illary had been the night before.

He was still glad that she was pregnant, but he wasn't sure which way a jury trial would go. He didn't have much to lose, though. Being imprisoned away from Illary was a special form of torture, and he knew that KSM wouldn't let him visit his child. All he could hope for would be quick processing of his paperwork so he didn't have to rot in an Intaran cell.

He gripped his rod and thought about Illary some more. He remembered the way that she had felt when he had released into her while taking her virginity. He thought about her hair, and the smiles that she gave him when they were in bed together.

He tugged on himself in a business-like fashion to release the nano-bots into the container that Xerxes had given him. He didn't like it, but he understood the necessity.

When he was done, he closed the container. He zipped everything up and knocked on the door.

"You can have the nano-bots back now."

The door opened a crack, and Xun gave the container back to Xerxes.

"I'm sure that all of this will be resolved one way or another soon."

"Thank you," he told Xerxes. Xun didn't bear any grudges against the messenger. It wasn't Xerxes' fault that Xun had violated KSM rules.

Reunion

Illary

The door of Illary's room clicked open. Illary looked at the door, and she sprang to her feet when she saw Kaley come through it. She nearly tackled Kaley with joy.

"You're here! And alive." She looked down at Kaley's stomach. "You're pregnant!"

"Yes. And from what I hear, so are you."

Both of them were crying tears of joy, and they wiped their tears away with identical gestures. Illary had forgotten how good it was to be around her older sister, since she'd been gone for so long.

"You have to help Xun. The Intarans are keeping him and..."

"I promise you that I'll listen to everything you have to say, but we definitely need to move you to better accommodations first." She winked at Illary. "No worries."

Kaley brought Illary out of the

building. When they got outside, Kaley pointed at the mountains.

"Those mountains are above the royal tunnels." Kaley spun and pointed again. "That way is the Great Sea."

Illary was twisting her hair in the way that she always did when she was stressed out.

"You don't care about Intara, do you?"

"I'm so worried about Xun that I can't really think about anything else."

"We'll see what we can do. Let's eat some lunch."

Kaley brought Illary to the kitchens, which were filled with wonderful smells of herbs that Illary had never seen before.

"How do you feel about apfelstrudel?"

"Sorry? What?"

"Intaran apple pastry."

"Oh, I'd love some." Illary had lost her appetite for a while now, but now that she was back together with Kaley, she felt like she could eat again.

"Where is Suyana?"

"Phuoc and Suyana were delayed, but they are still on their way. They should come any minute now. A solar storm pushed them off of their path, but they'll come soon enough."

Illary thought that she might not be able to eat the apfelstrudel after all. She picked off a tiny piece and ate it.

"If you're fine with Phuoc and Suyana being together, why is it so bad that Xun and I were together?

Why are we separated like this? Do you stay away from your own mate?"

"I know that you think that you are in love with Xun, but love is a very big thing. He's the first attractive man that you've ever been in contact with as a woman."

"He's my life mate. You know that he is, too."

"I know no such thing. Suyana will say the same thing to you. We can talk about it with her."

"When?"

"Right about now. We should go

to the space docks."

Kaley and Illary finished off their apfelstrudel before walking to the space docks. Illary felt a weight she didn't know she was carrying lift off of her shoulders when she saw Suyana getting off of the ship. Kaley and Illary both ran to her, and the three of them embraced, together at last after years of imprisonment and separation. All of them cried, but the tears were happy ones. None of them could speak.

Their reunion was interrupted by

an Intaran guard standing beside them and coughing loudly. They dried their eyes and looked at the intruder.

"Yes?" Kaley said, her voice as haughty as a queen's...which Illary supposed she was now.

"Your presence is requested, ma'am." He saluted her.

"Very well." She turned back to Illary and Suyana. "I'll catch up with you two later. Feel free to go anywhere you like in the royal tunnels. They'll know who you are. Our hair is a very excellent indicator of our kinship. Don't stray from the tunnels that have light crystals, okay?"

Illary and Suyana nodded. "We'll make sure to stay where we need to stay."

Shopping

Illary

Illary and Suyana linked their
arms as they walked back to the royal
tunnels. Kaley apparently had official
royal duties that she needed to do, so
they were free to do whatever they
wanted. Kaley had done very well for
herself, apparently, if the royal family
could afford to light their hallways
with jewels.

"I have a secret," she told

Suyana. It wasn't really a secret. She was just bursting to tell Suyana the news that she was pregnant.

"Ooh! What is it?"

"I'm having a baby."

Suyana immediately touched Illary's stomach. "You have a little baby bump!"

"I do. The baby is growing much faster than a normal Kadorian."

"It'll be fine," Suyana said immediately. "You're a healer. If anything's wrong, you'll know."

"I hope so," Illary sighed.

"Although I don't have much experience with this kind of thing..."

Suyana patted Illary's arm. "We can learn, no fear."

They were in some kind of indoor market now, the vendors selling pretty things. Many of the things on Intara glowed, which jacked up the price for new tourists just like Suyana and Illary. Illary didn't buy anything even though she still had Xun's credit pass, because she didn't know how she'd carry it all back to the palace. It would be better to wait for Kaley.

The sense of complete freedom on Intara was totally new. She might never say it, but she was glad that Suyana was with her, otherwise, it might be overwhelming.

Everything on Intara was just beautiful. She knew that she might never leave. It was hard to imagine the Alhmanic temple when she was surrounded by cheerful Intarans with their light hair; some people had light pink tints in their hair. She loved it.

Suyana went to a table and

grabbed a little locket. "Isn't this pretty?"

"Very."

"I have a secret, too." Suyana bit her lip.

"What is it?"

"I tried to kiss a boy."

Illary blinked at her. It was strange that Suyana had experienced anything outside of Illary's watchful supervision. She needed to get used to it, but she definitely missed their bond. Not so long ago, the two of them really only had one another.

"Who?"

"Phuoc."

Illary's blood pressure went up. She bit back her response; Suyana wouldn't want to hear it.

"But he wouldn't allow it. Guess he's not really my one true mate."

Illary felt her muscles relax just a bit. Suyana was so innocent. Illary felt as if she'd grown up a lot in a short time, and she could see the same maturity in Suyana. She used to be Illary's shadow, but she'd soon insist on standing on her own. With

Illary becoming a mother, maybe it was time to cut Suyana loose to let her learn her own heart.

Illary frowned. She knew her own heart now; she was old enough to choose her mate. And she knew that Xun was that man for her. She needed to hunt down Kaley and make her see it. She could clearly see the parallel between her situation and Suyana's, but Illary had gone much further than Suyana had.

"Go find someone to take you to a room to rest, Suyana. I'm going to find Kaley. Xun's in prison."

"Prison? Why?"

"Because of the baby. Violation of protocol."

"Oh." Suyana's eyes were wide. "I see."

Suyana walked with Illary back through the tunnels. They finally found a bot that could take Suyana to the royal quarters so that she could get some rest. Illary asked the bot to guide her to Queen Kaley, and it took her to a meeting room.

Cacophony

Xun

Outside of Xun's door, a heated argument was going on. The door muffled the noises, but he could hear a deep voice that sounded calm and in charge.

Then the door to his cell opened, and Xun saw an Intaran man with a circlet on his head. Xun bowed to him.

"Your Highness." He might finally

be free.

"Xun." The prince inclined his head. "I'm here to take you to a levi-car."

Xun nodded. He was more than ready to leave his cell.

The prince brought him out of the office, past all the guards who had kept him locked up at KSM's request. They got into a luxurious levi-car which Xun couldn't fully appreciate while worried about his fate. Then they were getting off on the pink Intaran plain.

"Where are we going?"

"The royal tunnels." The prince walked forward, and Xun followed him. As they got closer, Xun could see the opening to the tunnels. Near the entrance, there was a room, and the prince took Xun inside of it.

It was a meeting room with a conference table. Inside, there was a man and a woman with Illary's red hair.

"You must be Kaley."

Kaley nodded.

"Illary's in another chamber. We

have business to discuss. Primarily the business of how a KSM officer managed to get my sister pregnant."

"It wasn't planned. We went through a lot together, and now we are desperately in love. I've never fraternized with anybody before Illary. I know that it looks suspicious, but I truly believe that Illary is my lifelong love."

Kaley sighed. "I'm a romantic. I want to believe you."

The door burst open as Illary walked through and went straight to her sister without looking at anybody else.

"Kaley, I need to be allowed to see my mate for my own emotional well-being. I am with child, and it really is not your place to get involved with my mating. I have been trapped nearly all of my life inside of the Alhmanic temple, and I don't want Intara to be a prison, too."

"I don't want Intara to feel like a prison for you, either." Kaley sighed. "I wish that you'd guard your heart better, but I guess you can make your own choices. I remember you as a little girl, but you are a young woman now."

"I am. Xun is the most respectful and caring individual I've ever met in my entire life, and we are mates."

Xun cleared his throat in the corner. He couldn't believe that Illary was taking charge like this, letting her sister, a queen, know everything that she was thinking. "I love her, too." Illary beamed at him, and he felt like he was filled with warmth.

"Well, it seems as if both of you

are in love. I can cautiously give you my blessing. Since I'm the one who commissioned the extraction, I'll tell KSM that the mission was resolved to my satisfaction." Kaley sat back, and the prince with the circlet was near her.

"We will let you go provisionally; you are welcome on Intara, though we cannot make decisions for KSM."

"Understood."

"You can't go off-planet."

"No problem."

"Then we're done here."

Everyone stood, and Xun walked to Illary to give her a gigantic hug.

"Thank you for having faith in me," he whispered in her ear.

"I never doubted you."

"Let's get out of here."

The two walked into the royal tunnels. Xun might not be totally free, but at least he wasn't imprisoned in a cell any longer.

Celebration

Illary

"What should we do? Intara seems like it has so many wonderful things, but I've already gone shopping with Suyana."

"I was going to attend a champion sparring match, if you'd like to join me. We have our royal box, of course." God-King Jesaja's invitation seemed harmless, but Illary got the impression that he wanted to keep an eye on Xun.

Turning to Illary, Xun said, "You're okay with it?"

Illary nodded.

"Sounds like fun. We'll accept." His arm was still around her. They followed God-King Jesaja and Kaley out of the conference room. Jesaja brought them to a large levi-car outside. All of them got inside of it, and Illary realized that Kaley must have a fortune in order to send KSM to rescue Suyana and Illary and afford the levi-car. However, she wasn't jealous. She'd found something in Xun that Kaley had found in Jesaja, and love was worth far more than any amount of money.

The levi-car dropped them in an arena that was already packed, and then Jesaja brought them to the royal box. Illary didn't like watching fights all that much, but she stayed there for Xun's sake. When the final bell rang, everybody walked back to the levi-car.

"I might go into fighting...if KSM drops me."

Illary hoped that he wouldn't go into sparring matches — champions often had lasting brain damage — but she supposed that sparring might be safer than his work as part of KSM.

"We would like to invite you two to dinner."

"We'd love to accept. Just give me time to get dressed." Illary wasn't remotely dressed to have dinner with a God-King.

"Don't worry, we're dining as a family with the royal family of Saarland, but it's completely informal, I promise."

The levi-car brought them back to the royal tunnels. They walked through a set of tunnels that seemed to have different colored jewels than the tunnels that Illary had explored earlier.

"Our tunnels connect to the Saarland tunnels, since Jesaja's temple city is inside of Saarland," Kaley explained. "We have close ties to Prince Valdemarr and Princess Nina, so we eat with them at least once a week."

They made their way to a large chamber that had an enormous circular marble table with soft chairs stationed all around it.

Illary sat down in one, and the rest of the group sat down, too. The bots began to move forward and put food on the table.

"Let's wait for Valdemarr and Nina."

The door opened, and Prince Valdemarr and Princess Nina walked through the door, a dozen children in tow.

"My goodness!" Illary put a hand over her fluttering heart. "Are all of those children yours?" In Kador, a big family was considered five children.

"No," Princess Nina laughed. "The royal family takes care of the children in the area, and once in a while we do a big palace sleepover where we read them stories and put them to bed in order to give their parents a rest. Tonight is one of those nights. I'm tired from running around and playing a million games, but I always love these sleepovers."

"I love them, too!" A little girl with slightly pink hair hugged Nina's leg. "I like palace sleepovers!" She let go of Nina's leg before running a complete circle around the room and then selecting a chair. She stood on the chair and then jumped down.

"Me, too!" The children stampeded towards the table.

"Behave yourselves," Prince Valdemarr warned. "What will our new guests think?"

The little girl jumped into Illary's lap, startling Illary, who leaned back a little.

"Hello!"

"Hi."

"My name is Ermelinda. What's yours?"

"Illary."

"That's pretty! Are you going to live here?"

"Yes, I think so." Illary looked to Kaley for confirmation; Kaley nodded.

"Cool!"

Ermelinda wiggled out of Illary's lap and went to resume jumping from her chair. She had the attention span of a butterfly.

Illary hadn't been around small children in the temple, but as she watched the craziness of what seemed like a million kids running around the room, she admitted that she'd love to spend more time with them…which was a good thing with the baby inside of her.

"Maybe we should babysit the children, too, for practice," Xun said, leaning over to speak softly in Illary's ear.

"I was thinking the same thing."

She smiled at him and gripped his hand so she could squeeze it.

The dinner was a sumptuous but casual feast, the kids eating quickly before heading into a playroom supervised by Princess Nina. Xun and Illary had eaten until they were stuffed, and both of them had a hand on their stomachs, groaning from the abundance of food.

Dinner was certainly a welcome change from the tension of the days before. Xun twined his fingers with Illary's, and she looked at him. She could see in his eyes that he was comfortable and happy here on Intara, and maybe he'd be comfortable being here forever.

"I'm exhausted," Xun said, a beautiful light in his eyes. "I'd like to rest."

"Of course," Kaley told them. "I'll bring you back to your rooms. The bots do all the cleanup here."

She brought them back to the royal quarters inside of Jesaja's realm, and then she said, "Good night."

"Night." Xun and Illary waved goodbye, and then they were alone.

Another Vision

Xun

Xun got naked immediately. He'd enjoyed spending time with Illary's sister — although where Suyana had been, he had no clue — but now that he was free, he could go back to spending time with Illary.

Naked time.

He stripped Illary of her clothes, and then they were skin to skin again, reunited at last. He kissed her throat, her hair, her neck, her shoulders, every bit of her that he could find. He had her sit on the bed so that he could kneel on the floor beside her and taste her sweetness with her thighs over his shoulders.

"Oh," she moaned, her head tilting back, her back falling until she softly hit the bed. "Oh."

He continued to explore her with his tongue as she shivered in front of him. Her taste was so sweet that she was almost like sugar, sugar to which he was addicted. She orgasmed in front of him finally, her hands pushing his head deeper into the space between her thighs. When she was done orgasming from his tongue, he stood up and turned her over. Her feet were on the ground, but her stomach was on the bed. He stroked himself once, twice, and then he put the tip of his cock against her entrance.

"I missed you," Xun said, breathing heavily.

"I missed you...Oh!" Xun had entered her while she was speaking.

He could smell the scent of her arousal filling the air, sweeter than any perfume. Her red hair was a total mess behind her, since her head had thrashed around while she'd orgasmed the first time.

Thinking about the way that she'd clenched her thighs around him made him shoot inside of her, filling her with his sperm and nano-bots. He pushed her body against the edge of the bed so that her clit would be stimulated, and she convulsed hard as she orgasmed and returned his nano-bots to him.

She was still breathing hard when she told him, "That last orgasm made me have a vision. A small one."

Xun pulled out of her body. "What's wrong?" He pushed a strand of hair behind her ear.

"Nothing."

"I don't believe you." He kissed her neck softly.

She heaved a huge sigh. "Remember how I saw a temple falling in the Holo Sea?"

"Yes."

"I just saw a bunch of toppled temples. I don't know what it means."

"You don't have to worry about the Alhmanic temple; you're safe on Intara."

"I don't know why I keep seeing it, but it might be symbolic. If the Kadorians rebelled against the Alhmanics, they could probably bring the temple down by sheer force of numbers."

"You think that the rebellion would be successful?"

"The Kadorians have ancient

earth magic that draws on the heart of Kador. I think that they could expel the Alhmanics if they really worked together."

"Then we'll see if we can help them. I don't know if they could regain control, but someone could certainly try. I'm frankly surprised that the Intergalactic Federation hasn't interceded; part of the Alhmanic ability to avoid reprimands from the IF lies in not having a planet, but they essentially have Kador now, which means that they should answer to the same

authority."

"I agree."

"We'll figure it out, Illary." He

kissed her cheek before they fell

asleep on the bed.

Dropped

Xun

The next day, Xun was sweating as he waited for the verdict from KSM. Xerxes walked into the room and handed Xun a tablet.

Xun looked at the official notice in his hand. "I'm done with KSM?"

"Yes. There will be no official reprimand, since the client didn't care, but we can't keep you." The liaison nodded. "I don't think that you'll mind much, though. Your mating announcement ceremony will be soon, right?"

"Very soon," he said and nodded. He hadn't arranged it with Illary yet, but he was sure that Kaley would want them to formalize their mating in front of witnesses soon.

"You're staying on Intara?"

"As long as she'll have me." One door closed. Another door opened. Being dropped from his lucrative job at KSM was worth it. He could find another way to serve. By all rights, he did violate KSM's rules, because fate would bring him to Illary and Intara.

Xerxes shook his hand. "I wish you the best of luck."

Xun watched as his past walked away from him, and then he walked away without paying attention to where he was going. When his feet stopped, he looked up. He was in front of the office where he'd been held. Xun swallowed hard, and then he went inside.

"Hello."

A neatly dressed receptionist with

glowing Intaran skin and pink hair looked up at him. "Hello. How can I help you?" Life was a lot easier on the other side, that was for sure.

"What are your requirements for enrollment in the guard?"

She pulled out a folder of paper. "We have a lot of forms for the application process. You have to be thoroughly checked and have solid references."

"Why do you have so many paper forms?"

She shrugged. "The ancient way

of handling applications has been passed down through the centuries. There's no real reason why the Intaran guards all carry machetes, but it's part of the official uniform."

Xun wasn't sure about joining the guard, which seemed pretty small in scope compared to KSM, but he took the big stack of paper anyway.

"Thank you for these forms." He bowed to the receptionist, who inclined her head slightly. Xun went home to Illary.

When he entered their chamber,

Illary got to her feet and kissed his cheek.

"Where have you been?"

"I had to meet with Xerxes. KSM is letting me go. I have an application to join the Intaran guard."

"That's wonderful...you'd stay on-planet."

"Yup."

She stood on her tiptoes and tilted her face up, and Xun bent his knees a little and kissed her hard on the mouth. He put his hand on her growing baby bump.

"You and the baby are my future. I would sacrifice anything to keep the two of you happy and safe."

Emerald

Illary

SEVERAL MONTHS LATER

Illary felt like she would pop at any moment. Her back hurt all the time, and her ankles were swollen. She was only marginally cheered up when her sister Kaley came into her room with a mug of xocolatl. She'd craved it constantly during her pregnancy.

"Thank you for the xocolatl,

Kaley."

Kaley rubbed Illary's stomach. Kaley's new baby was resting in the nursery near her quarters, and Illary would put her baby in the same spot. Jesaja's priests were only too happy to look after the newborn children, since Intaran fertility was very low. Children were a blessing and a miracle.

"I have a question."

"Go for it."

"Did you ever have strange dreams when you came into your

powers? Lately, I've been having some visions that seem to be of the future."

"Let me think." Kaley crossed her arms and stared at the wall. "I did. I dreamed that I was performing in front of large crowds, but I didn't know what I was doing. I think that those visions were connected to my first performance on Intara, telling me that I'd meet my mate then. I don't do illusions all that often anymore, since I help Jesaja rule the temple city."

Illary was quiet. Her dreams were

telling her what would come. "I've been seeing falling temples."

"What does it mean?"

"No clue." She didn't know what would be strong enough to conquer the Alhmanics on Kador, but she'd help the rebellion if she could.

She felt wetness surge between her thighs.

"Kaley, I think my water just broke."

"Let's get you to the healer." Kaley quickly darted out of the room and came back with a gurney that was levitating. She helped Illary get onto it, and then she directed it through the hallways to the healer's hall.

The healers helped Illary out of the gurney, and she told them, "Call my mate Xun." He'd joined the Intaran guard and was on duty, but they'd kept him close during his mate's pregnancy, especially since nobody knew when Illary might deliver the baby. They re-dressed Illary into a gown which would give them the access that they needed while they delivered the baby.

A few minutes later, Kaley and Illary turned to the doorway as they heard footsteps. Xun burst into the room, slightly out of breath.

"Did you have the baby yet?"

"Not yet," she said, holding out her hand to her mate. "We were waiting for you."

He squeezed her hand as her eyes closed. The Intarans had some kind of vibrating device which helped her muscles push the baby out, but she tried to remember all the classes that she'd been through to prepare for this day. Kaley had had a very simple delivery, and Illary hoped that she could push this baby out with the same ease.

"Ah!" Illary felt her lower opening tear a little bit.

"The baby's head is out. One more push."

Illary gave it everything she had, bearing down. A healer was reaching between Illary's legs now, pulling the baby out of Illary's body. A different healer quickly cut the umbilical cord, and the baby was placed into a little sonic chamber to clean all the fluid off.

Soon, the baby was clean. A healer quickly slapped the baby's bottom, and the baby let out a surprised yelp.

"Good to go."

The healer wrapped the baby in a soft blanket before handing her back to Illary. The baby's eyes were closed as she nuzzled into Illary's shoulder. Illary felt her heart swell with love for her tiny child.

"You two are the most beautiful women in the universe."

Xun kissed the baby's little head, which was mostly covered in black hair with some red streaks. "She smells so good."

Illary could smell the baby's sweet scent, too. The pain of labor and delivery had been absolutely worth it. She felt like she ruled Intara at the moment, full of power and wonder.

The baby opened her little eyes when she heard her father's voice.

"Uh?"

"Come here, little one." Xun picked up his daughter, who had golden skin just as he did. She cuddled into her father's strong body.

"She has my eyes."

"Your eyes?"

"Haven't you ever noticed that my eyes are so dark that they reflect the color around them?"

"No."

"Take a look."

Illary looked at her baby as Xun bent down to show her eyes.

"Her eyes are pure, brilliant green."

"It's just the blanket." Xun shook his head. "She'll take on whatever color is near her eyes."

"Is this something from your side?"

"Yes, some of the Zhongguoren have chameleon eyes like I do. What shall we name her?"

"We should name her after the color of her eyes. Do you think that we should name her an Intaran name? Smaragd is their word for emerald."

"No, I don't want my daughter to be named Smaragd. How about the Kadorian word? What's the word for emerald?"

"Umiña."

"That's a pretty name."

"It's decided. Our baby girl will be named Umiña."

He settled the baby back in Illary's arms, and she felt a glow of warmth through her entire body, tired as she was.

"I love you," she told her mate.

"I love you, too."

THE END

About the Author

Would you like to hear news from Taylor Neptune? Sign up for Taylor's mailing list. Your address won't be shared with anyone else. Taylor doesn't like spam, and you can unsubscribe at any time.

Click HERE.

Afterword

Kador is deeply inspired by my time in Ecuador. While I was there, the Chevron-Texaco case was all over the newspapers. More than one of my professors had us watch Crude, a 2009 documentary about the pollution of the oil companies in Ecuador. One of my teachers was actually my professor's TA, and he had personally worked on the case as a soil technician. Until that day, I thought that it might all be spin. But he showed us aerial photos of the area where Chevron-Texaco had been, and everything there was black where only a few years before everything had been green.

I have to admit that we Americans aren't quite as bad as the Alhmanics, but watching that movie really brought home for me how much stuff happens outside of the United States to which we don't pay attention.

I am someone who thinks that the conditions that American

livestock live in are horrible but eat the meat anyway. I know where the oil comes from and how many innocent people are exposed to carcinogens as a result, but I drive my Ford car anyway. There aren't easy answers when you're used to living a middle-class American lifestyle. I think that awareness is the first step. What I tried to show with Illary was the view from the outside.

www.ingramcontent.com/pod-product-compliance
Lightning Source LLC
Chambersburg PA
CBHW060809030726
47503CB00002B/416